Addison Chained

Victoria L. Hicks

ISBN: 979-8-218-92686-1 Victoria L. Hicks

Cover Design by: Kevin Hicks

Printed in the United States of America

AUTHOR'S NOTE:

This book contains situations that could trigger some people, such as rape, kidnapping, physical and psychological abuse. This was inspired by a true story I heard many years ago but the details were never released, and at the time I wondered what really occurred in the untold nightmare behind the news blurb. Of course, I've taken wild liberties with it, and none of what follows is true or based on anyone real. It is rather a cautionary tale. BTW, no animals are harmed in this book… only people (and some of them really, *really* deserve it).

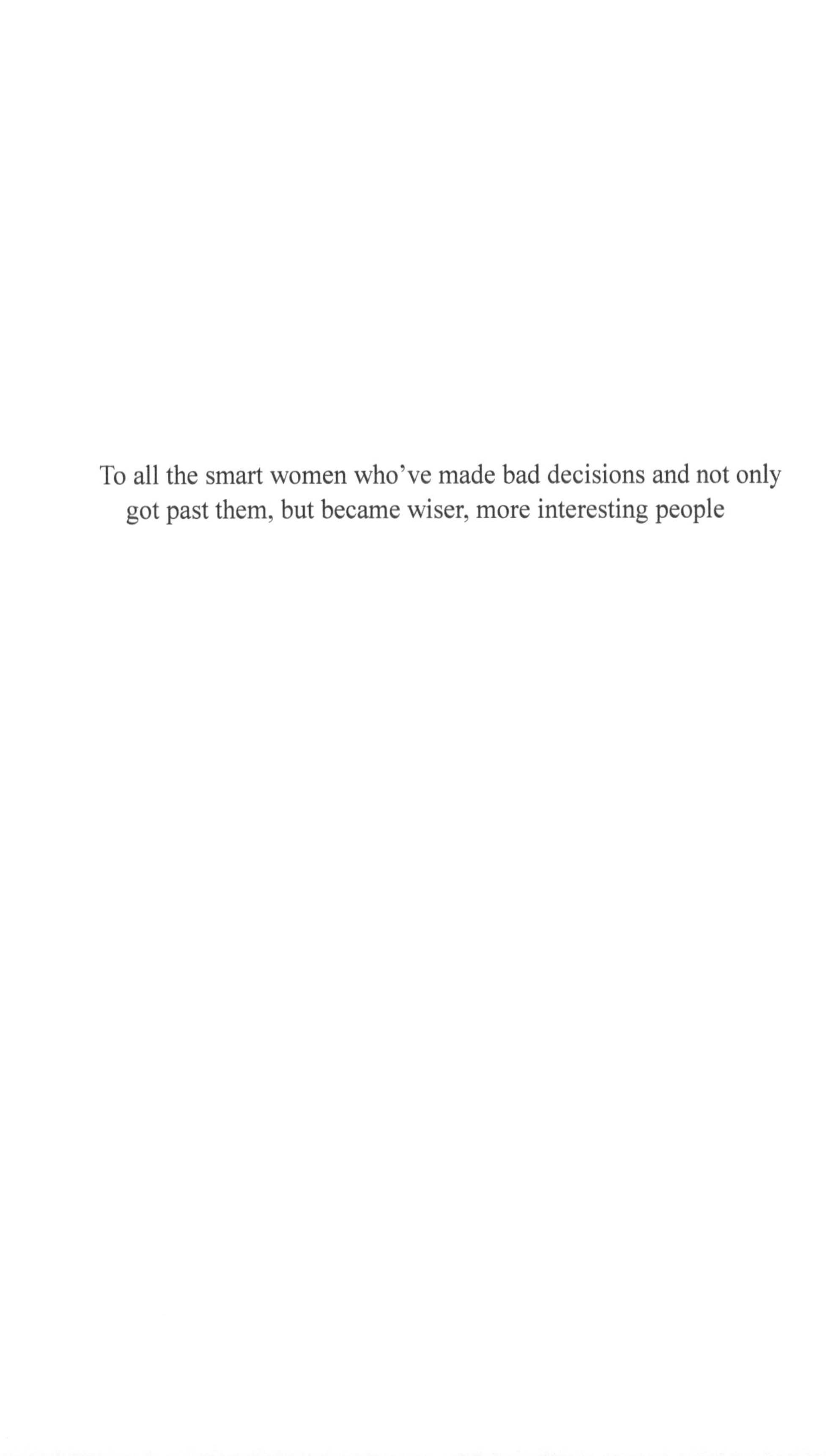

To all the smart women who've made bad decisions and not only got past them, but became wiser, more interesting people

1

Addison

I was naked and vulnerable.

The room was in semidarkness, lit by a single dim bulb from a lamp in the far corner. It was an impersonal space, uninviting and devoid of warmth. The furnishings had been chosen for an eye to efficiency rather than taste. The bedspread was thrown back, and I lay there waiting for him to appear with a mixture of anticipation and dread, my heart pounding furiously.

My arms were pulled over my head, cuffed to the headboard. The right one felt tight and it cut into the flesh of my wrist.

I was scared as always, and it was hard to breathe; my breath came raspy and harsh between my lips, sounding like it belonged to someone else.

I heard a door being opened.

Shit!

Suddenly he was standing at the foot of the bed, looking down at me. I did not know this man, he was a complete stranger to me. A slow smile spread across his face. I watched him slowly undress, my heart pounding against my ribcage. I pulled at the confining cuffs, but they firmly held me prisoner.

I looked at his lean naked body. He was sinewy, and a tattoo of a wolf stared at me with feral hunger. He crawled onto the bed and came slowly forward until he was almost straddling me.

He slid one hand up my thigh and it disappeared inside me.

He bent down and touched his lips to my ear. “You like that?”

I gasped loudly and turned my face from him, screaming inside.

Suddenly he grabbed my long hair and wrenched my head back, forcing me to look into his face. I gasped again from the sudden pain of his fierce grasp. He shifted again, his free hand continuing to probe me.

“How about that? You like that?” he wanted to know.

I stared back at him defiantly, my eyes narrowing with fury and disgust, and yanked at the handcuffs again.

“Struggle all you want,” he said softly. “It’ll do you no good.”

He leaned in and flicked my lips with his tongue. I tried to turn away again, but he grabbed my chin and forced me to look at him. He leaned in to kiss me.

I took his lower lip between my teeth and bit down hard!

“No kissing,” I said around my teeth and his flesh.

His eyes went wide with surprise and I released his lip.

“Don’t try that again,” I said firmly, then writhed under his continued touch. I closed my eyes and groaned, then looked back at him. “Finish it. Now.”

It wasn’t a request.

He laughed softly and moved to fulfill my command.

2

Addison

Sex is an addiction for some people. Not me. I don't even particularly enjoy it anymore. I use it to torture myself. That's why I always request the rough stuff.

I'm not completely stupid, though. I make sure it's safe. The online site I use requires both parties to have a safe word you can use to stop things at any point. I haven't had to use it yet, though I came close once.

I know hooking up with strangers is dangerous. However, it's the only way I can lose myself. And I need to lose myself because I can't stand being me, I can't stand my life anymore.

The hookup I had last night went predictably. We finished and he uncuffed me. I dressed and left, feeling dirty and debased as always. Despising myself as always. Yet in that brief time we had together I was able to forget everything — and I have so much to forget.

The minute I got home I got into the shower and scrubbed at my body, like I always do. Even so, I never really feel clean after one of those meetings. I did sleep well though, that kind of rough and tumble sex takes exertion.

Mornings after almost feel like nothing happened the night before. I go through my usual routine, get up, get dressed, have coffee and toast, then leave for work. Same ‘ole same ‘ole.

I was in the office at my computer, going over end of quarter reports, when a heavy hand landed on my shoulder. I didn’t give a startled jump though, I knew who it was.

“I’m hungry,” a voice whined.

It was Barb, my co-worker, and also my best friend since childhood. She was the one that got me the job at Jergins & Company as a bookkeeper. I loved her, but sometimes she could twang my last nerve. Like that very minute.

“You’re always hungry,” I said, not bothering to look up from the computer.

Barb sat on the corner of my desk and leaned toward me. “It’s past noon already,” she persisted. “Come on, Addy, let’s get outta here and grab something. It would do you good. You’ve been glued to that thing since you got here. I don’t think you’ve even gotten up to pee.”

“I brought my lunch,” I said.

“So eat it for dinner. Or feed it to your dog.”

“I don’t have a dog.”

“Then I’ll take it home and feed it to mine.”

I glanced at her. “You don’t have a dog either.”

She grinned at me. “Come on, Addy.”

I sighed and turned to her. “Look, Barb, I’ve got to get this P&L finished by the end of the day. I don’t have time for this.”

“Work, work, work.” Barb punched me lightly in the shoulder. “You need to get out and live a little, girl.”

If she only knew.

I crossed my arms and looked at her. “Don’t think you know everything about me, Barb, because you don’t.”

She raised her eyebrows. “Oh, really?” Then she smirked. “Yeah, well… Don’t think you know everything about me either.”

“Oh, really? Like what?” I asked, amused.

“Like…,” She leaned in and whispered, “I’m thinking about getting a dog.”

I laughed.

Barb’s always been able to make me laugh, even during the worst time of my life. I turned back to the computer and started typing again, but the smile remained.

Barb threw up her hands. “Okay, okay. Killjoy. Forget lunch, but we’re going to have drinks after work, and I won’t let you say no. I’m buying,” she added as a further enticement.

It was my turn to raise some eyebrows. “You never buy,” I retorted suspiciously.

“There’s always a first time.”

“Okay,” I finally said reluctantly.

“Okay.”

When she remained seated on my desk and didn’t move, I stopped typing and looked at her again.

“I said okay,” I said, exasperated.

She just threw me a wide grin and got up. At the doorway she turned and said, “I’m holding you to it. You’re not weaseling out this time. Five o’clock sharp.”

She sauntered out of my office without closing the door. I heard her call over to another coworker, but I didn’t catch the words. Probably giving the start of a victory speech. Look! I managed to drag poor Addison back into the world. Huzzah!

I shook my head. Even best friends can be a royal pain in the ass sometimes.

3

Barb

I've known Addy for a long, long time, and I knew she was going to try and duck out on me, so I parked my butt outside her office at five o'clock sharp. Sure enough, I watched as she slipped through the door and headed quickly for the exit. I wasn't gonna let her get by me that easy.

"Not so fast!" I called.

Startled, she looked over and I waved, grinning. She frowned.

"Nice try," I said. I walked over and hooked an arm through one of hers. "Let's go."

I walked her out of the building and down the street to Tony's Bar. Opening the door, I gestured her in. "After you," I said sweetly.

Addy rolled her eyes. "How very thoughtful," she grumbled, but she stepped inside.

Success!

Look, I know I sound like the world's worst busybody, but I'd been really worried about her. She had withdrawn from everyone, and she never did anything anymore but work or hide inside her house. Hell, I couldn't get her to do anything! I continually invited her to go out, but she always refused and wouldn't be budged. She wouldn't even meet me for breakfast on the weekends like we used to do. And even though I barge into her home unannounced all the time, she's so quiet and morose I can't take spending more than thirty minutes at a time with her, so I end up leaving. Anyway, I could always tell that if I didn't leave she'd come up with an excuse to boot me out.

I wasn't sure what to do.

Addy's been my best friend since grade school, and I love her, even though she'd become such a stranger lately. She was really more like my sister than a friend. We always seemed to know what the other was thinking, and I could usually predict what she'd do before she did it, and vice versa. We'd been through everything together, good and bad.

The bad was really bad. She suffered a terrible tragedy a few years ago. I was there for her then. I stood by her during that awful time and throughout its fallout. She was absolutely devastated. But I really assumed that time would heal things for her, like it does for most people; however, as the years have passed she's just became worse. She's transformed from an intelligent, funny, energetic woman into to an uncommunicative introvert.

Tonight I was determined to change that if I could.

I had a little surprise in store for her. I was pretty certain she wouldn't be thrilled, but the worst thing that could happen is she might haul off and punch me. It wouldn't be the first time. We've had more than our share of those girly fist fights since we'd known each other, the first one notably occurring in the second grade playground where we first met.

We wove our way through the crowded bar and miraculously found two unoccupied seats next to each other at the bar.

"Tony!" I yelled across the roar of the din. "Two margaritas!"

Tony, a heavy set middle-aged guy with a perpetual frown nodded gruffly at me from behind the bar. However, when he saw Addy slide onto the stool next to me, he actually smiled. She had that effect on people, mostly men. He actually walked over to us.

"Good to see you, Addison," he said. "Been a while."

"Hey, Tony," she greeted him with a smile. "Make mine a whiskey. Jameson."

He knocked on the bar counter in acknowledgement and took himself off to fill our order.

I never knew how she did that. She was pretty, certainly. Her beautiful long blonde hair was a magnet to begin with, and that coupled with her pale creamy skin and sea green eyes were enough to attract men and make women hate her. Not me, though. I knew my red hair, freckles, biker chick attire and loud demeanor didn't compare favorably, but I have risen above such petty comparisons. Well… not really… but I was used to being second fiddle to Addy. Anyway, I made up for it in personality.

"Since when do you drink whisky?" I demanded.

She peered at me from the corner of her eye and smiled. "Like I said, you don't know everything about me."

"Bullshit, I do, too."

She didn't argue.

Tony brought our drinks and I clinked her glass with mine and tasted my drink. God! I love margaritas! That salty, sweet lime thing was created by an absolute genius!

I looked around at the crush of people. "Look at all these delicious men," I cooed and nudged her elbow. "You know what's more fun than filling spreadsheets, Addy? Filling bed sheets."

She shook her head. "Not interested, Barb."

"In sex?"

She knocked back her finger of whisky and looked at me. "In anybody here."

"Come on!" I cajoled. "Look around. There's gotta be one guy in here that gets your juices flowing."

She shook her head. "Not interested."

"How do you know if you don't check out the field? That's how the game works, hon. Can't get mated if you don't move your piece."

She made a face at me. "That's a stupid analogy, Barb."

Frustrated, I slurped back a good swig of my drink and turned to look at her fully in the face. "Okay, we have to talk."

"Not again. Please."

"How long are you going to mourn?" I demanded.

She snapped her head in my direction, her eyes narrowed. "Barb…," she replied tersely, warning me off.

She quickly turned from me and caught Tony's eye, tapped on the bar next to her empty glass, and held up two fingers. He nodded.

"No. I mean it. It's been three years. It's time you moved on."

A pained look took over her face. "Please don't."

I knew I was upsetting her, but I continued anyway. "You're alone too much, Addy. It isn't healthy. I bet you haven't been on a date in years."

"How do you know?"

"I *know* you. You go to work and play with your nasty numbers every day, then sit home alone every night."

She turned away from me. "I like being alone."

"No one likes being alone all the time," I continued relentlessly. "There's a sea of men out there, why don't you take a dip?"

"I like my life the way it is," she replied tonelessly.

"Bullshit." I scanned the room. "Hey! Look over there!"

She followed the direction of my gaze. "What?"

Then she saw it. Or rather, saw him. A man in his thirties was looking back at us. He was tall and well built, with blonde hair and brown eyes. Noticing our attention fixed on him, he wove his way through the other patrons to us.

"Hi, Barb," he greeted me.

"Hey, Gary" I replied brightly. I gestured to Addy. "I'd like you to meet a friend of mine. This is Addison Clifton."

Gary smiled. "Hi. Nice to meet you." He had a nice, mellow voice. At least, I thought so.

"Hi," she retorted, giving me a dirty look.

I expected that reaction, but I bravely carried on. "Gary works tech support at Saunders down the hall in our building. Weird, huh? Been our neighbor all this time and we've never run into each other before."

"You obviously have," she said through her teeth.

Tony set down another whiskey in front of her. It was a double this time. Addy picked it up and drained it in one shot.

"Whoa!" I cried. "Slow down, soldier."

She whirled around to face me. "Can I talk to you in private for a moment?"

Uh-oh.

All I could do was say, "Sure." I turned to Gary. "Order yourself a drink and save our seats. We'll be right back."

He nodded and smiled, mostly at Addy. I slid off my stool, and she immediately grabbed my arm and hauled me through the crowd to the front door.

"I can't believe you!" she spit out at me.

"What?" I asked, playing dumb.

"You're trying to set me up."

There was obviously no use pretending. I threw up my hands. "Okay. Guilty as charged. But, come on, you need to join the living again. Celibacy is overrated, Addy."

"You know I hate that shit," she hissed. "I don't like being manipulated."

"Fine. But what's so wrong with meeting one guy? Just talk to him, that's all."

"I'll meet my own guys. Just stay out of my love life, Barb. It's none of your business." She opened her purse, pulled out her wallet and dug out some cash, which she shoved at me. "Pay for my drinks."

"Addy —"

Without another word she swung the door open and disappeared outside.

Well shit. That could've gone better.

4

Addison

I could've slapped Barb back in the bar, I was so pissed off.

I shouldn't have been surprised though, it wasn't the first time she'd tried to hook me up with some guy. What did surprise me was the fact that she kept trying, even though she had to know by now what my reaction would be.

However, as I made my way back to our building and the parking garage I started to cool off. I knew her meddling arose out of genuine concern for me, and as I got into my car I reflected that I was actually very lucky to have someone who cared about me.

I'd never known my biological father, he left my mother, Alice, not long after I was born. She raised me for several years by herself, then met and married Paul Clifton. Sorry to say he didn't particularly like me. I don't think he liked kids, period. I think he only legally adopted me for appearance sake.

My stepfather wasn't physically abusive in any way, but he wounded me nevertheless. It wasn't his aloofness, or the fact that he ignored me as much as possible growing up, but it was his usurpation of my mother. He demanded all of her time and attention, and she rushed to meet that demand. My mother took care of my immediate needs, but she saved all her affection for Paul. Which left me feeling abandoned and lonely. If it hadn't been for Barb, I would have been sunk in misery.

As a child I was bewildered, and tried all kinds of ways to get her attention. When I hit my teenage years, those attempts became louder, more contentious and more destructive. It didn't work. In fact, Paul took me aside one day and said if I didn't straighten up, he'd kick me out of his house. I could tell he absolutely meant it.

So I learned to be invisible. Any requests to my mother were necessities and nothing more, and I stopped trying to gain her love.

I studied hard and entered college a year earlier than most of my classmates. Ironically, by the time I graduated, Paul left my mother for his secretary. Devastated, she reached out to me for comfort, but it was too late for me. For one thing, I recognized it as a selfish move on her part, and for another I possessed very few feelings for her anymore – she'd destroyed those years before. I listened to her during her anguished calls, but offered no comfort or advice. She probably wouldn't have listened if I had anyway.

Not a stupid woman, she soon realized the bridge between us was broken, and the calls became fewer, then stopped for a while. A year later she remarried. Her new husband was Mike Jenkins. I met him once, and he actually seemed alright. He was a quiet, genial guy, which was perfect for my mother; she grabbed the reins and ran their lives with an iron fist. Maybe it was a knee jerk reaction to having been under Paul's thumb all those years. I didn't know, and didn't care.

Alice and I almost never talk anymore. Even when I was blindsided by tragedy three years ago, she didn't call, didn't offer condolences or try to comfort me. Which was probably a good thing, it would have only sent me deeper into the dark abyss. And I was in a *very* dark place.

But Barb was there.

Through all those years with Paul, and every one after, she'd stood by me, offering me the love and closeness we all need and crave. I don't know where I'd be without her in my life.

However!

I wished to hell she'd stop trying to tell me how to live my life!

It was infuriating, *especially* because I had such a close relationship with her. It was hard to make her back off without feeling like a crummy friend.

I got home and stood in my living room, looking around. Everything was neat and orderly. I'd furnished my small house with taste, but kept it minimal. It was easier to keep up that way, and I needed and craved orderliness. My home was the one space where I had total control, and control over the small things in my life was all I felt I had left anymore.

It was quiet, though. Too quiet.

I stood there, mulling over Barb's words. '*You're alone too much, Addy. It isn't healthy.*'

She was right, of course. I knew it wasn't a great way to live, but I couldn't help it. I needed my autonomy. The thought of getting emotionally involved with anyone again made my heart skip, and I'd break out in a sweat. I couldn't face a serious relationship with another person, other than Barb of course, but that was different.

I grabbed my phone and plopped down on the sofa. I scrolled to an app and tapped. The *HookedUp* site came up and I logged in. I had a lot of notifications on my profile page and I opened them.

They were pictures of different men. I went through them one by one, swiping each one to the left to indicate my disinterest.

Then I stopped on one. The man was attractive, although that wasn't necessarily the most important criteria for me; I needed to feel an immediate connection. This man had a captivating smile that was infectious, even hinting at a little danger there, and he looked straight into the lens, as if he were looking directly into my own eyes. There was something in his that almost seemed to be challenging me. *Go on, I dare you*, they seemed to say.

I took up the gauntlet.

I swiped his picture to the right, then sat back and waited.

A few minutes later I got a notification.

It was a match.

Then a message from him popped up.

Him: Doing anything tonight?

Me: Depends.

Him: On what?

Me: On you

Him: What do you want to know?

Me: Are you rough and kinky?

There was a long pause. Then….

Him: I can be anything you want.'

I sat back again and thought a moment. I could feel a small smile fight to break the surface of my reserve. I sat up again and typed.

Me: My safe word is…Mommy.

Him: I'll definitely remember that.

5

Addison

I was sitting on the bed. I'd been waiting for over thirty minutes, and was about to give up on him when there was a knock on the door. As I rose I wondered, not for the first time, if I was crazy to be doing this kind of thing. Almost every time I did it I'd tell myself that this would be the last time, but then I'd do it again anyway. Like I said before, I wasn't an addict, but deep depression has a way of changing you, and in my case I'd become reckless. A part of me wanted safety, but another part just didn't care anymore. That part almost welcomed danger, then at least I'd feel *something*.

I opened the door.

The man from *HookedUp* was standing there. He matched his picture pretty well. He looked to be in his mid-thirties, and he was really handsome in a quirky kind of way. His tussled brown hair was on the longish side, his eyes were light grey punctuated by little black specks, and at present he wore an engaging smile.

"Hi," he said in a friendly voice.

I looked directly at his face. "6'4"?" I challenged.

He smiled even wider. "A slight exaggeration. Is it a problem?"

No, it wasn't. It wasn't the first time a guy had lied to me about himself. Besides, he was still taller than me. I stepped back. "Come in."

He stepped inside and looked around the motel room. Like most inexpensive motels, it was designed with a desperate corporate attempt at cheery comfort that somehow came out a generic uniform drab. He turned as I passed him, watching me carefully.

"My name is — "

I cut him off. "No names," shaking my head firmly.

He gave me a long, indecipherable gaze, and suddenly I began to feel uncomfortable. "Do you want something to drink?" I asked, trying to keep my voice and hands steady. "I brought a bottle of whiskey."

"Sure," he said.

He watched quietly as I removed the paper covers from two glasses and poured the drinks. I handed him a glass and we both drank in silence.

I took a deep breath and said, "Just so you know, I need to make sure of safety."

"I know. Your safe word's 'Mommy'."

I shook my head. "The other kind." I walked to the small table in the corner, opened my purse and removed a couple of condoms. "This kind of safe."

He threw me a crooked smile. "Kinda weird, isn't it?"

"I don't think so."

"No, I mean, you don't want to get pregnant, but your safe word's 'Mommy'."

I tossed the condoms to him and he deftly caught them. “I’m more concerned about disease. And speaking of safe words, what’s yours?”

This time when he smiled he showed teeth. “Daddy.”

I tried not to roll my eyes. “Fine.”

“Do you do this often?” he asked me.

I poured myself another whisky and tossed it back, then stepped back and began to undress.

“Did you come here to talk or to fuck?” I asked.

Still smiling, he shrugged, sat his glass down and said, “We don’t have to talk.”

6

Addison

The old photograph was of my family. Matt and I were on the beach, and sunlight flecked the ocean waves behind us. A breeze was blowing our hair, and we were both laughing, giddy with the warm sun and sea air, and secure in our love for each other. In front of us stood Justin, holding up a seashell he had just found. Matt had one arm around me and another on our son's small shoulder.

I don't know why I tortured myself like this, but I couldn't help it. I kept the framed picture closed up in the drawer beside my bed because I couldn't bear to look at it every day and night, but there were times like now when I was inexorably drawn to it. I had to touch it, hold it in my hands, and look into the eyes of the man and child I'd lost. I wanted so desperately to see them one more time, to feel Matt hold me in his arms, to hear Justin's innocent laughter, a carefree bright sound that lit up our home and my heart.

I left the motel an hour ago, and as usual felt nothing but remorse as I sat in my too quiet bedroom, feeling lonelier and sadder than ever. This was almost becoming routine, the horrible need of my lost family coming on the heels of one of my sordid trysts.

I clutched the picture to my chest and lay on the bed, curling up in a fetal position, and when the tears came they were fiercely torrential.

The next day was Saturday. Weekends weren't easy for me. I felt too listless to join one of Barb's invites, but I couldn't just sit around either, so I decided to throw myself into a deep cleaning session. Not that there was really anything much to clean; like I said, I kept my house pretty minimal, so not a lot of dusting or that sort of thing, but I really needed a distraction. So I threw myself into reorganizing the kitchen.

I pulled every single thing out of the cupboards and set about re-categorizing everything. I can get manic about that sort of thing. Barb thinks I have a mild form of OCD, but I don't think it's that mild when I do things like this. I spent over two hours sorting and reorganizing everything, then turned my attention to the appliances. I scrubbed and polished, even resorting to using a toothbrush at times. If anyone walked in I'm sure I would have looked a little crazy.

On the heels of that thought I heard the front door open and slam shut.

"It's me!"

A minute later Barb entered the kitchen. She took note of my disheveled appearance and the fact that I was wearing rubber gloves and still clutched the toothbrush, which looked a bit mangled.

She grinned. "Cleaning again?"

"Yep."

She sighed and crossed her arms. "Still mad at me?"

I removed the gloves, brushed away a stray lock of hair and smiled. "I'm not mad. Come in."

"I'm already in."

"Then get yourself something to drink."

She glanced at the clock on the wall. "Well, I guess it's afternoon somewhere in the world." She headed for the cupboard where I usually kept my alcohol, but when she opened it all she saw was boxed goods. "What the hell?" She grimaced at me. "Now I'm going to have to relearn where you keep everything. I bet you did it just to mess with me."

"Not a blip on my mind." I tossed the gloves and toothbrush in the garbage. "Anyway, I didn't mean that kind of drink. Make some coffee while I get cleaned up."

I washed my hands and face in the bathroom, then ran a brush through my hair. As I gazed at my reflection, I saw that I looked tired. Not the kind that results from hard work, lack of sleep or worry, but the kind that depression causes. It's exhausting to be sad all the time. There were dark circles under my eyes, and my face looked pale and drawn.

When I entered the kitchen again Barb was pouring a healthy jot of brandy into her cup of coffee. She smirked at me and lifted the steaming cup like a toast.

"To our imaginary dogs!" She drank.

"So you found my stash," I said with a smile as I opened the cupboard over the fridge and took down a bottle of whiskey.

"Why'd you put it way up there? I almost had to get out the footstool. Afraid you have a drinking problem, and are trying to make it more difficult to get at?"

I laughed. "No, just changing things up."

"You need a hobby," she snorted.

I poured myself some coffee and added a small jot of whiskey to it. I sipped it slowly.

"Listen," Barb began. "I'm sorry about the other night."

"Forget it," I said, brushing it away.

"If it helps," she continued, "I got what I deserved. After you left, I went back and sat with Gary. Man, what a bore. You were the smart one to walk away. He somehow thought I'd be psyched about this new video game he's into. He sat there for a fucking hour detailing every boss fight, every cool weapon he used and every level-up. Definitely a hero in his own mind. I eventually played the headache card – which wasn't far from the truth – and ran outta there before I figured out how to kill him with a maraschino cherry stem." She added more brandy to her half empty cup of coffee. "I don't know what I was thinking."

I smiled. "You just have an inner yenta."

"I'm only a busybody with you. No, I think I'm just bored. I don't even really like bars anymore. I think I'm getting old."

I laughed. "I'll buy you a drool cup."

She poured more coffee, picked up the brandy and drifted out of the kitchen. "Just make sure there's a margarita in it. I still like those," she called back.

I followed. Barb plopped onto the sofa. My laptop was sitting open on the coffee table and she shoved it aside to put her drinks down. The movement brought the screen up and she glanced at it.

"Holy shit," she remarked with surprise, and her head snapped up to look at me. "HookedUp?"

I rushed over and quickly closed the lid.

"Oh, god, Addy, you're not on that site, are you?" She sounded genuinely concerned.

"It's no big deal," I said in a rush.

"Shit, Addy. This isn't like Tinder, though that isn't so great either. This is a dangerous site. It's for rough stuff. People have gotten killed from being on that."

I sighed, knowing I was in for another lecture. I couldn't explain to her that I was in a self-destructive mode, and that HookedUp was the only thing that seemed to be able to take me out of myself. She wouldn't understand. Hell, I barely did.

I tried to shrug nonchalantly. "It's just a game. Everyone gets a safe word. If it goes too far you can stop it."

"Oh, I see. It's not dangerous at all. Oh, no. But you need a fucking safe word so you can stop some maniac from choking you to death or whatever."

"You're exaggerating."

"You know nothing about the guys on that thing, but you hook up, just like that. At least in a bar there are other people around."

"I told you, I'm careful."

She reached over and grabbed my arm. She looked seriously worried. "Not careful enough," she said. "You're smarter than this, Addy. I had no idea you were doing this, and that's stupid of you. You should let someone know when you're going to meet one of those guys. It's a rule. Someone should always know where you are. And, of course, by someone I mean me."

I laughed sarcastically. "We're in the digital age, Barb, we're all already being tracked wherever we go."

She shook her head. "I mean it."

I wanted to be irritated, but I knew her nagging was coming from a place of love and genuine concern, and as I've already said I don't have many people who care about me.

"Okay," I said. "I promise, next time I meet up with someone I'll let you know where I'm going."

She narrowed her eyes, and I could see she thought I was just giving her lip service. "Addy…."

I made the sign of a cross over my heart. "I *promise*."

"Thank you." She sighed, took a large gulp of what was probably coffee flavored brandy by now, and sat back. "Girl can't be too careful these days."

I patted her shoulder. "Yes, she can."

Suddenly Barb laughed. "Well, at least I know now you're getting some action, and your girly parts haven't fossilized yet." She cocked an eyebrow at me. "I guess that's something."

7

Barb

I didn't trust her.

Addy was playing with fire going on that stupid site. I got a bad feeling, but short of staying at her place and sitting on her I wasn't sure what I could do about it. She'd already been through a lot, and I didn't want to see her hurt anymore. But she was right about one thing, it was her sex life and none of my business. Still, now that I was aware of what she was up to, I was sure I'd have plenty of worry ahead.

I somehow managed to get her to go to lunch with me. We went to a little French bistro nearby — going out was my idea, the restaurant was hers. I wanted to drag her to this great gritty little place that served amazing chili dogs, but I knew that wouldn't tempt her at all, so I agreed to her choice. The menu was on the frou-frou side, but I was able to order a hamburger and *pommes frittes*, so it wasn't too bad (except for that garlic mayonnaise shit they slathered on the burger). But the main thing was that I was finally able to drag her out of that goddamned house for a change.

Afterward, I dropped her off at her place and went home.

I was supposed to catch up on laundry, but I was feeling a little tipsy after all that brandy at Addy's and the two glasses of wine at the Frenchie place, so I plopped down on my sofa with my laptop and scrolled through social media for a bit, then looked up some real life stories about HookedUp.

I was right to be concerned.

Damn! Some of the things I read made my fucking skin crawl.

In one story, a young woman was taken by force, then repeatedly raped and beaten for twenty-eight days before she was rescued. In another, a man met up with another man, and his mutilated body was found later in a motel dumpster. Then there was a teenager who was kidnapped and trafficked as a sex slave for almost two years. Sometimes one of the parties went missing and were never found. Serious fucking Brrr. Not all were that bad, however; in many cases one of the HookedUp partners were robbed, sometimes of their life savings. Not that that wouldn't seriously suck.

God, the world was major ugly sometimes.

I was tempted to pick up the phone and call Addy, but I stopped myself. I'd already given her a lecture, so I doubted anything else I said would change her mind.

I just really hoped she'd stay true to her word and give me a head's up the next time she met up with one of those guys. I had my doubts, but I crossed my fingers anyway.

Again I heard the echo of her frustrated response to one of my diatribes on dating safety at lunch. "Why don't you focus on your own damn sex life, Barb. When was the last time *you* got laid?"

Well, as a matter of fact I did have a sort of boyfriend — well, more of a fuck-buddy to be honest, though I didn't say that to Addy.

All I said in response to her was, "Hey! I'm seeing a guy. And he's not some stranger I picked out at random on some website."

Luke *was* a decent guy, though, and we never engaged in all that masochistic rough stuff. I mean, who does that kind of shit? We even went to dinner together sometimes and did that sort of thing. *He* liked chili dogs, which was another thing in his favor. In fact, he's the one that turned me onto Dusty's Dogs. It was a big hangout for cops, and since he was a cop himself, he already knew how great they were. Plus, being with a cop made me feel safe — a lot safer than some hook up site anyway.

And Luke was seriously cute. He was really out of my league, so I felt lucky we'd bumped into each other and hit it off like we did.

Thinking about him made me pick up the phone to see if he was off duty that night. I figured I could use a wiener or two.

8

Addison

Despite her nagging, it actually felt good to go to lunch with Barb, so the next day I pried myself out of the house and went for a walk in the park. It was a warm sunny day with a fresh breeze, and large puffy clouds floated beneath a cerulean blue sky. I took some deep breaths as I strolled along the walk shaded by spreading tree boughs, and I was bathed in a sense of wellbeing I hadn't felt in a long time.

The park was full of other people who had the same idea. I passed by a mother and her teenage daughter who were in the middle of an epic argument about a guy named Eric. It made me smile, though there was a touch of sadness to it. My mother and I had engaged in similar fights when I was that age, but of course they ceased immediately after my stepfather's threat to kick me out. Mothers and daughters have to still be talking to each other to argue.

I passed a young couple who were sitting close to one another on the grass. He had his arm around her, and her head was nestled on his shoulder. I slowed, not taking my eyes off of them. I watched as he leaned down and kissed her. I turned away and quickened my steps.

The path curved, and as I walked along I began to hear the high pitched shrieks and laughter of small children. As I rounded the curve I found myself drawing near to a kids' playground. It was surrounded by a waist high fence and I stopped and leaned on it, watching them at play. I smiled at the joyful chaos as they ran, flew on the swings, and went down the slide. One kid was sliding down just as another one below was attempting to climb back up it. The boy coming down crashed into the other one and they tumbled to the ground, dissolving into raucous laughter. Their laughter was infectious, and I joined in, caught by their high spirits.

Just then a young couple entered the playground holding the hand of a small boy. The boy tugged at his father's arm, eager to join the fun. The laughter died on my lips and I suddenly turned away.

My good mood vanished, and it felt as if the sun rushed to hide behind a cloud. I trudged back to my car and drove home again.

I stood in the middle of my living room and gazed listlessly around. There was nothing to do. I had already cleaned and reorganized the place, so I was unable to forget myself that way. I turned abruptly, left the house again and drove to the nearby farmer's market.

I bought some fresh caught salmon off a small truck that sold seafood, some new asparagus, farm fresh zucchini and some tiny new potatoes. I stopped at the stall of a local vineyard and got two bottles of Reisling, and finally at a stall that provided fresh baked bread and pastries and got a small raspberry tart.

Loaded with my goodies, I returned home.

I loved to cook but hadn't done so in a while, so I threw myself into the calming routine of washing and chopping vegetables. I had soft music on and sipped wine while I cooked.

I set a place at the coffee table with a nice linen placemat and napkin, a small vase with a spray of roses I got at the market, a tapered candle and a clean wineglass. I was determined to treat myself, to try and recapture that first feeling of contentment I experienced at the park earlier. I turned the TV to a YouTube channel I liked, lit the candle and brought in my plate. I poured my second glass of wine and began to eat.

Halfway through I stopped and looked at my makeshift dining arrangement, which suddenly felt over the top and pretentious. The show I was watching had turned monotonous and uninteresting, and was quickly slipping into juvenile antics. I glanced at the empty places to my left and right. It was a sad, lonely show.

I took my half eaten plate and dumped the rest into the garbage.

***

There was a knock on the door and I got up to answer it. My previous match from HookedUp, the man whose safe word was 'Daddy' was standing there, wearing that same enigmatic smile I noted last time. He was holding a bottle of whiskey in one hand.

"Hey," he said.

"Come in," I invited and stepped back into the room.

He stepped into the motel room, grinned and shut the door behind him. He walked with feline grace until he stood next to me. He turned me around and encircled me with his arms and nuzzled my neck. I roughly shrugged away from him. I didn't like that, it felt too intimate.

My reaction didn't seem to faze him, though. The smile remained as he fished into a pocket of his jeans and withdrew a pair of handcuffs. He dangled them in front of my face.

"What do you think?" he asked.

"Hm," was my only reply.

The truth was I liked to be the one to suggest things like that, it felt safer somehow. And I wasn't entirely sure I was in the mood for that tonight anyway. I felt hollow inside, and I wanted intensity, not games.

"Don't you like to be tied up?" he asked, his mouth turning up into something akin to a small smirk.

"Sometimes," I said. "Not now, though"

"Okay," he said calmly. "Maybe we'll try them out later."

The sex was what I'd asked for — it was raw and frenzied, but not too much. I'd had rougher. Once finished, we lay sprawled across the bed, which looked like a tornado had hit it. I closed my eyes, once again wishing I hadn't done this, and once more vowing it would be my last time.

He got up and disappeared into the bathroom. When he returned he was carrying two glasses of whiskey. He sat on the edge of the disheveled bed and handed me one.

I sat up and pulled the sheet around my naked body.

He raised an eyebrow. "Not thirsty?" he asked.

I shook my head. "No."

"Ah, come on. You're not gonna make me drink alone, are you?"

I sighed and took the glass from him. "So, what're we drinking to?"

He raised his glass and said, "To new games."

I paused a moment, then shrugged and tossed down the whiskey. I sat the empty glass down and turned back to him. He just sat there, looking at me. It felt like he was waiting for me to say something, but I ignored him, got up and went to the bathroom. I peed, then washed my hands and face. Like I said, I always felt unclean after one of these little get-togethers.

I returned, gathered up my clothes and began to dress.

"So we're done here?" he asked. He didn't seem upset, just mildly curious.

I nodded and got on my panties and bra, but when I tried to get my legs into my jeans I kept missing somehow. Suddenly, I felt like my body was going numb and I had a hard time controlling my hands.

"Are you alright?" he asked.

I didn't answer because I couldn't, my mouth felt fuzzy and thick. I kept dropping my pants. As I reached for them a second time I realized my vision was blurring. I suddenly felt very tired, and found it hard to move at all.

He came and sat next to me. He held my chin in his hand, raising my face to his, and I couldn't resist. He looked into my eyes.

His face slipped out of focus, and I felt like I was falling. I wanted to cry out for him to catch me but I couldn't speak at all.

Then I fell, and suddenly there was nothing but a vast empty black void, and my consciousness slipped away as though I ceased to exist.

9

Addison

I opened my eyes and was met by a flickering light that hurt, so I immediately closed them again. I took several deep breaths and tried again. Everything was still blurry, but after a moment my vision began to clear, and I realized I was staring up at a single dim bulb hanging from a dark ceiling raftered by old beams. I felt horribly tired and groggy, and my muscles ached miserably.

"This isn't…," I murmured softly to myself, and was surprised by the thick slur I heard in my voice.

I was confused. I should be in the motel room.

Where the hell was I?

I turned my head to look at my surroundings and gasped aloud. Soft fingers of fear crawled up my arms and neck.

I was in a dark, damp room made up of cement walls and floor — a basement of some kind. I could feel something stiff and strangely tufted beneath my fingertips, a rough unyielding landscape beneath my body. I glanced down and saw I was lying on a bare mattress. There was something unsettling about it, as if it were a reflection of me, as if my life were suddenly made bare, exposed, and without protection just like that mattress.

That's when I suddenly realized I was naked.

I struggled to sit up and was abruptly overcome by nausea. I leaned over the side of the mattress and vomited. I felt a little better afterward, but became conscious of a terrible headache. It felt like I was suffering from the world's worst hangover. How much of that whiskey had I drunk?

One glass. I remembered now, I only had the one.

Panicked, I looked around, trying to find my clothes, but there was absolutely nothing I could use to cover my nakedness. Except for me, the mattress and a large discarded dog cage stowed in a far corner, the room was empty.

I was wide awake now, and caught in the firm grip of rising terror.

He drugged me, knocked me unconscious and brought me here, the man whose name I didn't even know.

Jesus fucking Christ!

I had to get out of there, and fast, clothes or no.

I struggled to rise when I heard a strange clanking sound. I glanced down and was shocked to see that one of my ankles was enclosed in a thick leather band. Attached to it was a chain. My eyes followed the chain up the wall to where it was anchored firmly by a large, sturdy bolt embedded in the wall.

I was being held captive!

Oh my god, oh my god, oh my god!

Barb had been right! How could I have been so stupid?

Irrationally, I began yanking at the chain, but it was firmly embedded in the wall. I tried desperately to tear at the leather anklet, but not only was it strong and thick, it was held closed by a small heavy lock that required a key to open it.

Shit! Shit! Shit!

I looked frantically around the room again. The far corners were shrouded in dark shadows. I looked to the ceiling. Running between the weathered wooden beams were old pipes and wires, dressed in the shredded rags of ancient cobwebs. That meant spiders. I shivered with fear and loathing, imagining a small convoy of them crawling up and down my naked body.

"Hello?" I called up to the ceiling, praying that someone upstairs might hear me.

My voice rang hollow in the dim, musty bare room.

I tried again. "Hello? Is anybody there?"

There was no response.

Panic completely took over, and in a wild voice I began to scream, "Help! Help me, somebody! Help!"

Then I thought I heard something and stopped. I sucked in my breath and listened intently, my heart thudding painfully against my chest.

There was the definite sound of muted footsteps overhead.

Then I heard the sound of a lock being turned. My head followed the sound and I noticed for the first time a narrow wooden staircase on my right. The top steps disappeared into darkness and I couldn't see where they led to. I heard a door being opened to the accompaniment of a whining hinge. For a moment there was no sound, and I listened breathlessly to a silence that felt oppressive and ominous.

"Is… is somebody there?" I called in a hoarse whisper.

My frightened inquiry was answered by the sound of a heavy footfall on the top step. Suddenly, I was terrified, afraid of who might be there. I shrunk in on myself as much as possible.

I watched as a man's legs slowly came into view, and when he reached the bottom I could just make out his features – it was him, my latest HookedUp guy. I wasn't surprised, but my fear was mounting and almost suffocating me. My heart felt like it might hammer its way out of my chest.

He just stood at the bottom of the stairs, staring at me with no expression.

"Where am I" I demanded, trying to sound braver than I felt. I yanked at the chain. "This isn't funny. How the hell did you bring me here? I told you I wasn't in the mood for stupid games right now!"

He smiled then.

I began to tremble all over, but desperately tried to still my hands and hide the shakiness in my voice. "You need to brush up on how all this works," I said angrily. "You can't just take me somewhere without my consent." I yanked on the chain again. "Not cool, dude. Unlock this. Right. Now."

He took a step toward me, still smiling that unsettling smile. "You need to say the magic word."

"Screw that!" I cried. "You need to do what *I say.*" I held out a hand toward him. "KEYS, asshole. Now."

He chuckled and shook his head. "My mattress, my rules."

I sat back against the chilly cement wall, drew my knees up and covered my breasts with my arms. I firmly shook my own head. "No. You agreed to the site's rules before we met. We both did. *Mommy.* It's my safe word, so you have to back off now." He just stood there, smiling. "Mommy-mommy-mommy!" I screamed at him. "Okay? Now get this thing off of me!"

He laughed in earnest. "That doesn't work here."

I began to pant with fear. I really believed when I went to HookedUp the men there would follow the rules. How utterly naïve!

I could plainly see that he wasn't playing anymore, that it was no longer a casual one and done kind of thing. He was deadly serious, despite the smile.

He began to slowly walk toward me, and for the first time I recognized the callous indifference in his eyes. It may have always been there, I just never bothered to notice before. After all, it was supposed to be just a one-time hookup, so I didn't study him very hard. Bad mistake on my part.

"No!" I screamed wildly. "Stay back!"

He stood right above me now, a dark menacing silhouette against the bare bulb behind him, his very stance radiating danger.

I shook so bad I couldn't control it any longer, and shrank as far back into the wall as I could, desperate to create distance between me and him. He bent down toward me.

Oh, shit.

10

Addison

I lay there, stunned and feeling broken. I felt my insides had been violently torn, broken, skinned and bruised.

Maybe I wouldn't be in so much pain if I hadn't fought so hard, which I had. The fear and rage surged up and I hit, scratched and bit with everything I had. So he hit me, more than once, until I was subdued.

It was very different from my previous HookedUp meet ups. Those had been rough and sometimes kinky, but I'd never felt this afterward — mental pain and guilt, yes, but nothing compared to the physical and mental trauma that engulfed me now.

Worse was how small and vulnerable and helpless I felt. I was trapped in a stranger's basement, and I had no idea where I was and no way to call for help. And he had just proven he had no regard for me at all. He raped me repeatedly and violently until I almost passed out from pain and shock. When he finally rose again, I felt so dirty it seemed all the showers in the world would never make me feel whole and clean again.

He pulled up his pants and leaned down again, and though his nearness utterly repulsed me, I was too numb to even turn my head. He ran a finger lightly down my cheek, and I shuddered at the touch; something about it was almost worse than the rape.

"Good girl," he whispered.

He went back up the stairs, whistling. WHISTLING! Then he was gone.

My stomach was empty or else I think I would've thrown up again. But I just lay there on my back, staring up at the pipes and cobwebs, feeling so incredibly stupid. And guilty. Some part of me felt that it was all my fault, which in a way it was. I should have called or texted Barb like I promised, but I'd been so cocky and sure of myself, and I resented having to check in and tell her where I was going as if she were my mom. Stupid.

Some lessons are expensive.

At some point the shock paralyzed and numbed me, and I fell into a troubled sleep. When I woke again there was a cold gray light coming into the room from a tiny window at the top of the wall across the room. For an instant I wondered where I was, then the memory of the night before washed over me and I sat up abruptly. I looked down at the bruises I could see, felt anew the pain in several places, and viciously tugged once more at the chain. It was hopeless.

"Gaaaaaawd!" I screamed, an animal howl I didn't recognize erupting from me.

"Don't exhaust yourself," said a quiet voice.

I whirled to see him standing a few feet away. He had come down the stairs so quietly I hadn't heard him. I immediately shrunk back against the wall and bared my teeth at him.

He was holding a tray.

"Let me go. Please." I said, desperately attempting to sound calm and reasonable.

He smiled, walked closer and set down the tray. On it was a sandwich on a paper plate and a plastic bottle of water. Nothing that I could use as a weapon.

"Eat," he said.

"Fuck yourself!"

He chuckled, seeming to find my retort funny for some reason. "Really," he said. "You need to eat." He pushed the tray closer with the toe of his sneaker.

I pulled the plastic tray closer and looked at the food and water. He'd drugged me at the motel so there was no way I was going to touch the stuff. I picked up the tray.

"Good girl," he said.

I flung it at him, watching with satisfaction as the sandwich fell apart — it looked like tuna — and the bottle bounced on the cement floor. I was disappointed it didn't explode.

"No way, asshole."

He looked at the mess with a sigh, then back to me. Then he shrugged. "Suit yourself." He walked back to the foot of the stairs, then turned. "But in future when you address me… you will call me 'Daddy.' Got it?"

The hairs on my arms stood up. Wasn't that his HookedUp safe word? It didn't phase me when he told me that at our first meeting, but now there was something horribly creepy about it.

I shook my head forcefully. "No."

He was across the room in two long strides and slapped me so hard my head was knocked into the wall behind me.

"There are rules here. You *will* follow them."

Then he was up the stairs and I was alone again, my head pounding almost as hard as my heart.

11

Barb

I knew I couldn't trust her!

When Addy didn't show up for work on Monday, I was concerned. It wasn't like her — she takes that responsibility thing way too seriously. Even when we were in school, she was meticulous about doing her homework every day, and showing up at every extracurricular activity ten minutes early and fully prepared. It was so irritating.

So the fact that she wasn't at work was uncharacteristic, but I knew she'd been depressed lately so I didn't worry too much at first. However, when I found out she hadn't bothered to call in sick an alarm bell went off in my head. That definitely wasn't like her.

I called her but it went straight to her voicemail.

Unfortunately, I got caught up in a bunch of stupid meetings throughout the day, so she was relegated to a back burner, but when I got off work I drove to her house. I knocked several times and when she didn't answer, I got the spare key she hid behind a loose brick and let myself in.

"Addy?" I called.

I gave a cursory glance in the kitchen and living room then headed for her bedroom. I mean, if she was sick that's naturally where she'd be. It was empty.

"Where the hell are you?" I asked the empty room.

I went through her place more carefully, trying to see if she'd left a clue to her whereabouts, but found nothing. I even opened her laptop, but of course it was password protected. Then like a dope I remembered to go check the garage, and I was relieved when I found it empty. That meant she was off somewhere.

But what was she doing?

Even if she'd taken a personal day she would have called in. That was Addy. She definitely would've let someone know she wasn't coming in.

Standing in the empty garage I thought again about her being on that HookedUp site, and wondered if that had anything to do with her truancy at work. Maybe she'd found a guy she really liked and decided to make a marathon of it. Though that sounded more like something I'd do rather than her.

However, she'd proven she was capable of surprising me. I never would have figured her for the type to go on a meet-up site like that to begin with.

I checked my phone again to see if she had responded to any of my texts, but she hadn't, so I gave it up and left, making sure everything was locked and the key returned.

But when she didn't show up or call on Tuesday I knew something was really wrong, and real panic set in.

I called and texted repeatedly and there was still no response, and another trip to Addy's house was met with the same emptiness. I could see nothing had changed, so she'd obviously never come back there since my last visit. Same glass in the sink, the laptop in the exact place as before, and the kind of stale smell that occurs when a place goes unoccupied for a bit.

Damn it! I knew, just *knew* she'd gone off on another one of those HookedUp things. And that bitch didn't tell me where she was going like she promised!

Now she was in trouble, I could feel it.

I immediately dialed Luke. He was a cop and so I assumed he would know what to do. He didn't answer so I suspected he was on duty. I left him a voice message, but I sounded so panicky and garbled I sent him a text that more calmly laid out my fear for Addy.

I debated whether to stay at her place or go home, then decided on the former. If Luke got back to me anytime soon he might want to see her place, and I wanted to be there to let him in.

Almost an hour went by, and I was getting ready to go home when my phone rang and I saw it was Luke.

Thank god!

"Luke!" I said in a rush.

"What's going on, Barb? Something about some friend of yours?"

"It's Addison," I said. "She's missing!"

"How do you know?" he asked. "Just because she hasn't returned your calls—"

"Luke, she's missing. She hasn't shown up at work for two straight days, she hasn't returned one of my calls or texts. That's not like her. I know her, she'd never just disappear like this unless something was really wrong. I'm very worried. Also, her car's not here."

He was silent a moment then said, "Maybe she went on a trip."

"Luke!" I almost yelled. "Addison is missing. I think something bad happened. You're a cop, can't you *do* something? It's your job, right?"

"Okay, okay," he said, trying to calm me down. "Yeah, I am, but missing persons isn't something I do. I'm just a patrol cop, Barb. If she's missing or you think she's been abducted, you'll have to talk to a detective from Criminal Investigations. That's not me."

Been abducted. It was the first time it had been voiced aloud, although I'd suspected all along that might be the case. But he was being so goddamned calm about it I felt like throwing my phone across the room. However, I'd just break my phone and not his face so I didn't do it.

I took a deep breath then said, "Fine. Can you at least refer me to someone? You gotta know one of those detectives, don't you? Can you at least give me a name?"

"I dunno. I think my partner knows someone over there, I'll check with her and get back."

"Can you call her now?"

He let out a little grunt. "Why don't you just go to the station and a detective will be assigned to you."

"Fine."

I hung up on him. Fat lot of help he was. What was the use of knowing a cop if they couldn't help in a crisis?

12

Addison

I lay deep in a dark well, curled in on myself, fearing to wake. Then I began to hear something, a noise that seemed to grow louder, penetrating my black cocoon. Almost against my will I swam toward consciousness.

I finally pried my eyes open.

Confused, I found myself in a new setting. I was no longer in that damp, dark basement, but in a small room. I had no idea how I'd gotten here. He must have carried me up while I slept. I shuddered at the thought of his touch, the idea he had had his arms around me.

I sat up slowly, feeling unnaturally groggy. It hit me then that he must have drugged me again somehow. I didn't know how he did it since I'd refused any food or water, he must have done something while I slept.

I was ruing the lack of water now though, I was painfully thirsty. My tongue felt swollen and was stuck to the roof of my mouth.

I made to move my hand when I realized I couldn't. I looked up to see that one of my wrists was handcuffed to a wooden headboard. I was also still naked, and feeling more vulnerable than ever. I tugged at the restraints but had no better success than I had with the chain in the basement. I finally stopped because the metal of the cuffs was cutting into my skin every time I jerked at it.

I looked around me. I was on a bed, and it was the only thing in the room. There was a window on the adjacent wall, but it had been sealed by heavy metal shutters that I could see were firmly screwed shut, cutting all access, but allowing razor knives of light in between the slats. The sharp lines of light and shadows cast on the opposite wall made the room look fittingly like a jail cell.

Suddenly, all the fear and horror came crashing in on me and I screamed, over and over again, dissolving into a flood of tears.

"Let me out!" I howled.

I was completely breaking down, but somewhere in the middle of my anguish I heard something. I thought it was the same sound that had roused me. I took a couple of deep breaths and tried to steady my convulsive breathing. I gulped and listened. At first there was nothing, then it came again. There was a faint knocking on the wall beside me.

I stared.

"Hello?" I called in a soft quavering voice.

There was nothing.

"Is… is someone there?" I whispered.

The knock came again, louder this time. I maneuvered so I could just lay my head against the wall. "Hello?" I repeated a little louder.

"Hello!" came a reply. It was a woman's voice.

My heart began to beat furiously, and I became so excited I started to shake.

"Please, help me!" I yelled. "I'm being held a prisoner, I'm handcuffed to the bed! Please, please help me!"

There was a long a painful silence on the other side.

"Hello?" I called urgently. "Are you still there?"

I was met by yet another long silence.

I was about to start screaming again when the woman on the other side of the wall answered. "I can't," she said.

"God, no!" I cried. "You can't just leave me here! He may come back any minute! Can you at least call someone? The police!"

After a few beats in which I held my heart in my throat, she said, "I'm really sorry, but—"

I totally lost it then and became more than a little hysterical. "You can't leave me here! I have to get out! I have to get out!"

"I CAN'T!" she shouted back. "*I'm* trapped in here!"

All the air in my lungs exploded from me like I'd been punched. I stared at the blank wall in shock.

"You're — what?" I asked in a small voice.

"He kidnapped me, too."

I suddenly felt numb.

"No," I whispered, then felt the hysteria and panic returning. "No, no, no. It can't be! This… game's gone too far."

"Game?" her muffled voice echoed in disbelief. "This *isn't* a game. He's deadly serious."

My tears returned. "Oh, my god," I moaned. "This can't be real."

"I'm so sorry," said the woman.

I sat there blubbering, wiping the tears and snot dripping from my nose, and because I had no other recourse, was forced to my hand on the pillow. I looked at the wet spot on the cheap fabric with disgust. Finally, I regained a little control and asked, "What's your name?"

"Cheryl," she replied. "Yours?"

"Addison." I paused, then forced myself to ask, "Did… Has he hurt you?"

There was a long silence.

"Yes," Cheryl finally replied.

Oh god.

"No!" I cried. "How did this happen? Things like this can't happen!" I waited but she didn't answer. "Hello? Cheryl?"

There was a soft rap on the wall and she called in a tense voice, "Shh! I think he's coming!"

I heard a small sound like a wounded animal, and I was shocked to realize it had come from me. However, I steeled myself, and pressed my head back against the wall and strained to listen.

I heard a door opening and being thrown back against a wall.

"Have you been a good girl?"

I shuddered. It was *him*.

"Yes, Daddy." That was Cheryl.

My stomach twisted.

There were footsteps, then the raspy squeak of bedsprings.

I heard Cheryl begin to whimper, then she pleaded in a scared voice, "Please…."

There was a loud thump against the wall and I jerked back in surprise.

"Come on," said *Daddy*. "You know the drill."

I put my ear to the wall again and heard a violent struggle going on, followed by a loud scream from Cheryl.

I pulled back and began to frantically yank my wrist again, trying to do something, anything, to somehow get free. Of course it was useless.

There was another scream from the other room.

I couldn't take it anymore. I started screaming too, my own blending with Cheryl's until I couldn't tell hers from mine. Something popped behind my eyes and they both clouded over, and once more I was falling into darkness.

13

Cheryl

I wondered who Addison was. I'd heard him bring her in the previous night. I imagine she was terrified. Of course, in her situation who wouldn't be?

He had talked of bringing someone new in, so I knew it was going to happen. I wish I could have prevented him taking *her*, but I couldn't do a thing to stop him, of course. He'd targeted her specifically, that I knew. I wondered why. Was she young? Beautiful? Malleable and easily tamed? I didn't know. I guessed I'd get to know her a little after a while… at least until she was discarded. Of course, I mean killed.

It was a horrifying situation we were in.

I am —or was before all of this — a mental health therapist, with a degree in psychology.

So I knew the type of men who kidnap and hold women in captivity have some common traits. It's usually not a psychological abnormality, but more often it's because these men have a desperate need for relationships and power.

Especially the need for power.

They're also narcissistic, and only see the world in terms of their own desires, completely without any kind of empathy for the women they hold against their will. They want all the attention, and in order to get it, they'll take a woman and exert complete control over her.

Daddy has a terrible mean streak as well.

I think he hates most women, and has a deep-seated need to retaliate against all of us. So he's chosen to kidnap and release that venom, knowing his captives can't fight back, which sets the scene for a nightmare world.

And, believe it or not, guys like him aren't someone you could easily pick out on the street. Men who did these kind of things were typically in their thirties, forties or fifties. Some of them seem like nice guys, and some are even charming, which makes it all the more of a shock when you discover who they really are and what they're capable of.

I met him at a bar and could never have guessed what he had in mind, or how my world would be so devastatingly upended. He was handsome and so damn charming. When I woke up in his house I was stunned at how easily I had been duped by him, and how vulnerable and helpless I felt.

I had been there a long time.

I couldn't say how long, I'd stopped trying to keep count and time almost didn't feel real to me anymore. I wasn't married or even had a boyfriend at the time I met him, but I'd left family behind, parents and a younger half-brother. I had a hard time even remembering what their voices sounded like anymore, and I wondered if they'd given up on me. Probably.

I could hear her crying on the other side of the wall. Poor thing. I wondered what he'd already done to her. I was certain I'd find out soon enough, that I would be witness to all kinds of brutality. Especially if she fought back. Daddy knew how to punish those that displeased him, and it wasn't pretty

14

Addison

I was woken by the sound of the door opening. I glanced at the boarded up window, and by the deep golden tone of the light coming through the shutter slats I guessed it was late afternoon.

"Do you need anything?"

Startled, I looked over to see *him* standing in the open doorway. I shied back immediately, pushing myself against the wall as much as possible.

"Do you need something?" he repeated.

"What?" I finally asked hoarsely, my throat dry and swollen.

Once more in a patient tone he asked, "Do you need anything?"

Seriously? "Did you really just ask me that?" I rasped.

He'd been smiling, but at the sarcastic bite in my voice his face darkened. "Maybe you need an education on how this all works," he said.

He started toward me, but I stopped him by quickly saying, "Yes, I do need something."

He stopped and gave me an inquiring look. "Well?"

"I… I have to go to the bathroom." I wasn't kidding. My bladder felt it was about to burst.

He studied me for a long moment, his eyes narrowing slightly, then he removed a small set of keys from his pocket and approached the bed. He leaned over me and I instinctively cowered, trying to push my body even deeper into the wall and away from him. He unlocked the handcuffs and stepped back. I gratefully rubbed my raw wrist.

"This way," he said and motioned to the open doorway.

I stood up and tried to cover my naked body as best I could with my arms. I took a step and he raised a finger, pointing it at me.

"I expect you to behave."

We emerged into a hallway. He had a hand around one of my arms and half guided, half pushed me forward. He stopped me at the second closed door. He opened it to reveal a medium sized bathroom.

"In there."

I sidled past him as fast as I could and quickly closed the door. I went to lock it, but there was none. Shit.

I heard him chuckle on the other side of the door.

Bastard.

I leaned my back against the door and looked around the room. My eye lighted on a towel hanging from a rack and I seized it immediately, wrapping it around my body. It made me feel less vulnerable, not much, but it was better than nothing.

My throat and mouth were so swollen I ran to the sink and turned on the tap, scooping the water in my palms to my lips, over and over, drinking until my thirst was finally slaked. Then I sat on the toilet and peed. The relief was immense.

My next move was to escape. My eye went to the window and my shoulders sagged. Just like the bedroom, it was barred by another set of strong looking shutters screwed into the frame.

"Shit," I whispered.

Outside the bathroom, he began to whistle. The sound grated along my nerves.

I went to the shutters and tried to pull them loose, but they were set far too securely. They wouldn't budge.

Outside the whistling continued along with a new sound. It sounded like he was twirling the set of keys around a finger. Like nothing was going on, no big deal, just another routine day in the life of a psychopath.

I turned to the medicine cabinet on the wall and was crushed again when I saw he'd removed the mirrored panes, so I couldn't use it as a weapon. I opened the cabinet, hoping against hope I might find something, anything, inside I could use. But it was empty.

Fuck.

I moved back to the shutters and put my eye to a crack. All I could see was a portion of a grass lawn. There was nothing else nearby I could see. I could be in an ordinary suburban home or an isolated cabin in the middle of nowhere for all I could tell.

There was a sharp rap on the door.

"Time's almost up!" he called.

I scanned the room carefully one more time, praying I had missed something useful to use against him, but there was nothing. He had planned everything to his advantage.

When I finally opened the door he was leaning against the opposite wall, twirling his keys and whistling that inane tune. He looked at the towel I'd wrapped myself in.

"Are you cold?"

A harsh laugh escaped me. "I'm a *lot* of things right now."

"Well," he pushed himself away from the wall and pocketed the keys. "We can certainly do better than that."

He took two steps and opened a closet door. He reached in and removed two long robes on hangers, holding them up for me.

"Your pick."

I snatched the closest one off its hangar and pulled it on, letting the towel drop to the ground beneath it. I gratefully belted it tightly around me and eyed him warily. He just smiled — again, like there was nothing in the world wrong — and turned his back to replace the other robe.

I reached over and slammed the open door into his back as hard as I could. It pushed him a little way inside, and I sidled past the door and full out ran.

He was after me in a flash.

I raced down the hall and erupted into what looked like a living room or den. I spied the front door and sprinted as fast as I could toward it, snatching at the brass doorknob. Before I could turn it, his arms were on me. He wrenched me violently away and tackled me to the ground. I punched and slapped and scratched at his face, drawing a little blood.

He slapped me so hard my ears rang, then pinned my arms down. We were both panting hard, staring into each other's eyes, both furious.

"I told you to be on your best behavior, didn't I?" he snarled at me.

He removed one hand and gave me another hard slap.

"Didn't I?" he demanded.

My vision blurred as tears filled my eyes, and I was disgusted he was seeing me cry like that. He rose, jerked me to my feet, then dragged me over to a desk that held a computer and a bunch of manuals of some sort. He yanked open a drawer, drew out a handgun, cocked it and placed it to my forehead. I froze immediately.

He leaned in, his face almost touching mine, and said, "Last thing I want is to use this to prove my point." He paused a beat, then said,

“But I will if you push me like this again.” I began to tremble, terrified. He lowered his voice to almost a whisper. “Rule number one… There are consequences for your actions.”

15

Daddy

Even when you're making a simple dish you have to do it right, you can't take shortcuts. I was making a pot of chili, but not the slop most people do. I carefully browned nice chunks of beef, then added freshly ground roasted chili powder, cumin and finely minced garlic. The aromatic smell of the spices rose in the steam as I stirred in water.

See, what most people don't understand is that real chili, the kind they used to make on chuck wagons, isn't ground beef, it's more like a stew — meat slowly simmered in a thick, spicy sauce. It was culinary genius. I intended to serve it with soft flour tortillas and a nice avocado salad.

She wouldn't be able to turn this down. I mean, she had to eat at some point, and I knew the aroma of this would more than tempt her. However, if she still refused to eat I'd have to force feed her like the geese they bred for paté, and that would be a shame, but I couldn't let her get too skinny.

I'd just covered the pot and turned the heat down when there was a knock on the back door.

I immediately reached for the butcher knife lying on the counter and carefully looked out of the window.

Shit.

"I know you're in there!" called a voice from the other side of the door, followed by a fusillade of further knocks. "Open the door!"

I stared at the wall, trying to tamp down the rising anger his presence always stimulated in me. Would that fucker ever go away and leave me alone for good?

I slammed the knife back down and walked over, unlocked the door and flung it open. I stared grimly at the grizzled old man who stood on the threshold.

"Are you gonna ask me in?" he asked, giving me what I'm sure he thought was an engaging smile. I wanted to wipe that smile off by punching him until his face caved in.

"I'm busy," I replied.

"Well now, that's just too damned bad," he said. "I need to talk to you."

He pushed past me and came into the kitchen. I closed the door and scowled at him. He'd never change, the son-of-a-bitch.

"Now is not a good time," I said gruffly.

"It never is with you."

"You think there might be a reason for that?" I asked sarcastically.

He pulled out a chair from the small kitchen table and sat down. I glanced at the basement door, making sure it was securely closed, then pulled out my phone, found a song and played it, raising the volume. I sat the phone down on the counter, the music blasting.

"Do you have to do that now?" he whined, covering his ears. "It's too damned loud."

"Too bad," I said. "What do you want?"

He sat back and regarded me, calculation in his mean old eyes. "How can a guy who works at home be so busy all the time, huh? Ain't the point of being your own boss being able to schedule things the way you want?"

"What – do – you – want?" I repeated more firmly.

He shrugged. "Can't a guy see his own son now and then?"

I made a scornful noise.

"How's your programming stuff going?" he asked.

"Don't worry about my stuff."

"Seems to me like they give all those apps and things away for free these days. How do you make money if they get it for free?"

My eyes drifted to the knife on the counter. I was itching to pick it up and plunge into his chest.

"Myself, I don't trust those things," he continued. "The government can track everything you do on them, did you know that?"

"Go home, Dad."

"Why? I just got here."

I'd had enough of him and his goddamned games. "How much do you need?" I demanded.

He tried to look affronted and I almost laughed. He was a lousy actor. He grimaced. "I don't like your tone."

"How much?"

Finally he dropped the act. "Couple a hundred should do it."

"Couple a hundred?" I echoed, shocked. "Didn't you just get your disability check? What the hell did you do with it?"

He had the grace to look sheepish. "Well, there was this thing…."

Furious, I spat out, "This thing? It's called the racetrack, dad."

He leaned toward me. "I tell you, son, I had a lock on—"

"Save it," I snarled and walked out of the room.

I marched into the living room to my desk. I pulled the ring of keys out of my pocket, unlocked one of the bottom drawers and pulled out a small metal box I kept cash in. I unlocked it, removed two hundred dollar bills, and slammed it shut again, making damn sure to relock the drawer.

Just as well I did. As I turned I saw my father scoot back around the corner. The little fucker had been watching me, making careful note of where I kept the money. I thought about the butcher knife again.

When I returned to the kitchen he was sitting in his chair again, trying to look innocent. I held the cash out to him.

"That's all you're getting."

He quickly reached out and snatched the money. "Sure, sure." He thrust it into the pocket of his threadbare khakis and narrowed his eyes up at me. "You know, you were always a little shit," he said, all pretense of being a loving parent gone.

I laughed sardonically. "Oh, yeah. *I* was the shit."

He stood up and tugged at his shirt. "Well," he said. "It's nice to know you finally became good for something after all these years."

He reached over and patted my cheek. I slapped his hand away.

"So long, kiddo." He strolled to the door, opened it, then turned and said, "See ya around."

"Fuck you, dad."

He just laughed and left.

I stared bitterly at the door, wishing with everything I had I could finally kill the old bastard.

16

Barb

I'd been waiting for almost fifteen minutes and was starting to get pissed. The fat guy manning the desk had been ignoring me ever since he'd told me to take a seat and wait. I kept looking at the time then stare back at him with a stern eye, but he pretended I no longer existed. I'd had enough.

I stood up and strode over to him. I looked down at his nameplate. Sargeant Wycowski. I rapped my knuckles on his desk. He looked up, his face expressionless.

"Is somebody coming or what?" I demanded.

Before he could answer another man joined us at the desk. He looked like he was in his early thirties, with a body builder's physique that his suit jacket and tie didn't hide very well.

"Ms. Meade?" he inquired.

"Yeah."

He extended his hand and shook mine. "I'm Detective Lemuche. Sorry about the wait. Come with me, please."

I followed Lemuche. I glanced back at Wycowski, but he'd picked up the phone and was speaking in a very low voice to the person on the other line. Even though he wasn't looking in my direction I shot him the finger anyway. Unhelpful prick.

Lemuche escorted me through a door into a large room full of separate desk setups. He led me to one by a window. There were two desks that abutted one another. Another man was already sitting in one of them. He looked older. Detective Lemuche gestured to him.

"This is my partner, Detective Kennedy."

Kennedy nodded at me. "Ma'am."

"Have a seat," said Lemuche, who sat down himself at the other desk.

I sat in one of two chairs nearby.

Lemuche picked up a writing tablet and glanced at it, then to me. "Sargeant Wycowski says you're here about a missing person."

Wycowski. I didn't launch into the diatribe I wanted to about him, instead I just nodded and said, "Yes. Her name's Addison Clifton."

I watched Lemuche write her name down. Kennedy did nothing, just sat with folded hands and regarded me carefully.

"What's your relation to her?" asked Lemuche.

"She's my best friend. I've known her since grade school," I answered.

"What makes you think she's missing and not gone off on her own somewhere?"

"She hasn't answered any of my calls or texts for two days now." I saw him make a face and rushed to add, "And she hasn't shown up for work. I work at the same place. She never called in either. Seriously, it's not like her at all. If you looked up the word *responsible* in the dictionary you'd find her name and picture. Plus, she lives by herself and would never jeopardize losing her job like this."

"Is her boss concerned as well?" asked Lemuche.

"Well, at first she was pissed, but I think that now even Sarah's becoming concerned."

Lemuche wrote something then asked, "When was the last time you saw her?"

"Three days ago. Saturday. We went to lunch together, and that's the last I've seen or heard from her."

Lemuche tapped his pen thoughtfully against the pad then looked up at me. "Have you seen any changes in her behavior lately, anything odd or seeming out of place where she's concerned?"

I nodded quickly and told them about Addy going onto the HookedUp site, and how upset I got when I found out. "She promised she'd let me know the next time she went, and would let me know where the meet up would happen."

"And did she?"

"No. But I think she went anyway."

"Why do you think that?"

I smiled wryly. "Addy's stubborn. She doesn't like people telling her what to do, not even me. Plus her car's gone, I checked." He asked me for the make and model but I didn't know. I don't know shit about car stuff. Anyway, they were the police, for god's sake, they could look that up. "I need you to find her, I'm really worried," I went on.

"We'll do what we can, Ms. Meade."

"Why don't you start by getting ahold of her messages to the men on that site, I'm sure the guy responsible for taking her is one of them."

"So you think she's been abducted?"

"There can't be any other explanation," I replied a little unsteadily. "You get ahold of her messaging on HookedUp and you'll find the guilty bastard."

A small smile appeared on Lemuche's face.

Detective Kennedy leaned toward me. “Although most dating sites cooperate in cases like this, they value their customers’ privacy. We’d need a court order or a warrant to access that.”

“Then get one, dammit!” I commanded.

He just looked at me with no expression.

Lemuche asked for Addison’s address, the name of our workplace, her parents’ names, and any recent pictures of her. I sent him several from my phone right then.

“I want to know the minute you find anything,” I said urgently. “Who knows what’s happening to her as we speak.”

17

Addison

I was looking through close set wire mesh at the basement beyond. Daylight was fading and it would soon be dark. I was curled up in a ball. It was the only way I fit in the dog cage he had locked me into after our fight in the living room.

There was a sudden thump and the cage shook.

I looked over my shoulder to see him standing at the back of it looking down at me. Once again I hadn't heard him come down. He kicked the cage again and I jerked.

"Are we going to behave now?" he asked calmly.

I nodded mutely.

He pulled out those goddamn keys and used one to open the lock that kept me imprisoned in the cage. I crawled out on my hands and knees, feeling humiliated and debased.

I got to my feet and saw with a huge sense of relief that he was holding the robe he'd stripped me of before. He held it out and I yanked it from him, hastily throwing it on and belting it firmly, feeling a small sense of security in having my nakedness covered again.

He turned me roughly around and pushed me toward the dark narrow stairs. He marched me up them, staying right behind, a large hand on the back of my neck. At the top I opened the door and the bright light made me blink momentarily, having to shield eyes that had been in the dark for too long.

I was pushed inside, and I felt him brush past me. When my vision finally cleared, I saw I was standing in an eating nook of a kitchen. However, my eyes focused immediately on the woman before me.

She was a tired looking brunette in her mid-thirties. She was sitting at a small table. Like me she was dressed in a robe, but what immediately caught my eye was the fact that one of her ankles had a handcuff around it, the other cuff was firmly fixed to one of the table legs.

"This is Cheryl," he said. "I believe you two have already met."

He shoved me forward and forced me into the chair opposite her. He removed a second set of cuffs from his pocket and quickly secured one of my ankles to the table in the same fashion as her.

Cheryl and I stared mutely at one another.

She was very pretty, with large brown eyes and high cheekbones. She looked at me intently, and I felt like she was trying to convey a message, but I wasn't sure what. It didn't matter though, she was obviously a captive like me. The only difference is that I was pretty sure she had been there longer than me. She looked so exhausted and defeated I wanted to cry.

"How about some chili?" Daddy asked, moving into the kitchen and removing bowls from a cabinet. "I make a mean chili."

I started to tell him to fuck himself, but Cheryl quickly gave me a warning look and subtly shook her head. I bit off the words, saying nothing instead.

"You have to be hungry, Addison," he said.

It occurred to me then that it wasn't the first time he had used my real name, and he shouldn't have known it. I went by my user name on HookedUp, and never gave him — or anyone I met there — my real name. So how —? Then I realized he must have gone through my purse after drugging me. Shit. Not only did he know my name now, he knew a lot of other things about me, things I wish he didn't.

"No," I began, then saw another warning look from Cheryl and stopped. "Yes, I am."

Cheryl nodded at me.

"Good girl," he said smiling. "You're going to need your energy."

A shiver went through me.

As he began to ladle the chili into bowls, my stomach twisted. I hadn't eaten in two days, though I'd bent enough to take water — I had no choice there. It was that or die quickly of dehydration. Cheryl was right, I decided. If I was going to get out of there I had to eat, otherwise I'd be too weak to escape. I continued to look at her until he sat a steaming bowl down in front of me. My nose quivered at the appetizing aroma.

He quickly sat another one in front of Cheryl, then sat himself between us.

"Dig in," he said, and picked up his spoon and began to shovel in a mouthful.

I looked down but there was no cutlery. I looked across at Cheryl, and saw her scoop up a piece of meat with her fingers and eat. Clever asshole! He wasn't going to trust us with anything that could be used as a weapon.

"Could I at least have a spoon?" I asked.

"Nope."

I looked down at the food and couldn't stand it anymore. I scooped out a piece — it was hot — but my stomach rumbled so I shrugged the pain off and shoved it into my mouth. It was delicious. I didn't know whether it was due to his culinary skill or to my fierce hunger, but I finished it in no time, and wished there were more.

He smiled at me, pleased.

The smirk on his face made my stomach turn.

18

Cheryl

A cat that plays with a mouse does so for several reasons. The mouse is ultimately its prey, and it toys with it to tire the mouse out. The cat isn't always driven by hunger, but does this for practice and honestly just for plain fun. It enjoys weakening its prey. It's also very exciting for the cat, the battle between it and the mouse fulfills a deep-seated instinctive urge to stalk and capture.

Cats aren't innately cruel — but some people are.

Daddy loved toying with his captives and deliberately causing pain. He was trying to exhaust Addison until she couldn't fight back, until she was too weak to resist his control over her. He would continue to beat her down until she was completely under his thumb.

Neuroscience research shows when a psychopathic person imagines or watches others enduring pain, there is an increased activation in the brain related to receiving a reward, while also a decrease in areas related to empathy.

I think that pretty much defined Daddy.

He enjoyed hurting women. I saw his eyes light up whenever he inflicted pain.

On the other hand, the prey mindset is very different. The prey is constantly watching, looking for threats to its existence. They are highly alert and pay close attention to the predator, trying to predict their every move.

Allsion was very much in the fight or flight mode at that time. I watched her struggle between lashing back at Daddy, then re-thinking her strategy and pulling back, like a mouse will freeze, hoping to be overlooked by the predator.

But as I watched her I saw she was also stubborn, and would fight back with everything she had. That could be a good thing in the end, but in the meantime she was going to royally piss him off, and I'd seen the kind of punishment he could inflict when a woman tried to thwart him. It was a very bad idea, and I tried to signal her at dinner to ease up, to remain passive. Otherwise, she would be in a world of hurt.

I knew that for a fact.

Several times during the meal her eyes would dart toward me in mute appeal, and it was hard not to feel for her. This must seem like a nightmare, and I knew she was very frightened, but there wasn't anything I could do chained to a table, now was there? So I tried to help her survive by giving meaningful looks and little nods, hoping she would understand. She seemed to, and she eventually calmed down and ate.

That was good. Daddy might be a psychopath and narcissist, but he was also an avid cook, and took pride in his culinary efforts. If she refused to eat the food he made there would be bad consequences.

But as I watched her I saw that she was also very smart. That was good. She had to learn how to play the game there or she wouldn't survive long, and I was glad at last to have someone else with me, even though it was in the worst kind of circumstance. I had been alone with Daddy for some time, and I was desperate for company — other than him. I craved the closeness of another woman, so I hoped and prayed she wouldn't step too far and get herself killed right away. He was certainly capable of it.

19

Addison

I was tired of being raped, which is exactly what happened after the meal.

He undid my ankle cuff, jerked me out of my chair and dragged me away. I looked back at Cheryl, who was looking down at her empty bowl, unable to meet my eyes. She knew what was coming next.

He hauled me into that hallway and tossed me into the small bedroom I'd occupied before. Without a word he yanked the robe away and threw me onto the bed. It was messy and rough, and I almost gagged at the thought he was inside me again. I turned my head away, unable to look into his face.

When he gave that final grunt, he buried his head in my neck while his breathing slowed and settled. Then he raised himself on one arm and looked down at me.

"Good girl," he murmured, then rolled off of me and left the room.

I just lay there a moment, squeezing my eyes tightly shut. Then I turned my head and fixed my eyes upon the thin beams of moonlight that slashed their way through the shutter slats. Beyond them lay a different world, a world where there was safety. A world where I could live without constant fear. A world where my body wasn't bruised and violated by someone who delighted in hurting me. I extended a hand toward it, toward that world beyond my reach.

I rose painfully to a sitting position and stared dully at the floor. Tears began spilling down my cheeks in the dark.

The next time I looked the moonlight had bowed to streaks of bright sunlight. I must've fallen asleep, though I didn't remember doing so. I lay on the bed, clutching the robe tightly around me, still staring at the slits of sunlight, when I heard the door open. I jerked myself upright, holding my arms across my body.

"Thought you might like some company," he said.

He was standing just inside the room, holding Cheryl by the arm. He let her go and pushed her forward, then closed the door. I heard a key turning in the lock.

Cheryl was clad in her own robe. In her hand she held two bottles of water. She looked at me uncertainly, then nodded to the end of the bed.

"May I?" she asked.

I nodded. She sat down next to me and handed me a water. I unscrewed the top and drank thirstily, draining half of it in seconds.

"Pig!" she spat out, unscrewing her own bottle. "*Company*, he calls me. As if I have a choice in *anything* here."

Something broke inside me, and I snapped out of the mental torpor I'd been stuck in. I urgently grabbed both her hands, spilling some of her water on her.

"God!" I croaked. "Oh, my god. I can't even believe this. How did this happen?"

She shook her head. "I wish I knew," she said tiredly. "I'd go back in time and prevent it."

"Did you meet him on HookedUp?" I asked.

She gave me a confused look. "What's that?"

"Oh," I said slowly. "It's a… a sort of dating site." Obviously, Cheryl had been smarter than me and hadn't messed around with that particular danger. It somehow made me feel even dirtier. "Then how did he get you?"

She hung her head. "I was stupid," she replied.

I was pretty sure whatever she did wouldn't compare with my own stupidity.

"I met him at a bar. We hit it off right away. He was charming and funny and… really handsome." She almost gagged on that last word. "We had a few drinks then… I asked him to my place." She finally looked up at me and gave me a lopsided smile. "Stupid, wasn't it? He was a complete stranger. But I was so attracted to him — and full of alcohol — that I wasn't thinking straight. Once in my apartment he urged another drink on me. I passed out almost immediately and woke up here and… well, you know the rest."

I glanced at the door and lowered my voice. "How long have you been here?" I whispered.

"I don't really know, I've lost all track. Long enough for anyone who cares about me to assume I'm dead."

I thought about that a moment. "Then… if you've been here this long, maybe he doesn't intend to kill me — us." I said slowly.

She shook her head. "Don't bet on that. I'm guessing once we're no longer fun he will. He certainly can't just let us go."

That chilled me. Because of course she was right.

She studied my face, then said, "You look young. That's probably why he took you." Tears sprang to her eyes. "Which means my time may be winding down. Oh, god… I don't want to die. Not here."

My heartbeat quickened at the thought, not only that he might do something awful to her, but that if he did it would just be him and me. I looked at her face and saw real fear.

"First, I'm not that young," I said, trying to calm her. "I just look it. And… and maybe he doesn't intend to… do anything like that. Maybe he just likes variety, and that's why he abducted me too." The thought made my stomach twist. Sick bastard. "And look at it this way; with me here, it takes some of the heat off of you."

I couldn't believe I was saying much less thinking those things, but I suddenly felt so sorry for her. She's been in this hell longer than me. I certainly knew the kinds of things she'd been through, or thought I did anyway. And she was right. He couldn't just let us go when he got tired of us, which meant there was only one alternative. I had been frightened the whole time, but now I could feel my earlier horror and panic returning.

Cheryl snorted sarcastically at my words. "He doesn't tire that easily. He's got stamina enough for two of us."

"Who is this guy?" I asked. "Have you found out anything at all about him?"

She shook her head no. "He's keeps everything close to his chest. He's just a crazy psychopath — who's fucking both of us now."

I dropped my head in my hands. "Maybe he's fucking you," I said, "But he's raping me."

I heard her gasp and looked back up. She was looking at me with wide eyes. "Did you just really say that?" she asked in disgust, wiping at her tears.

"God, I'm sorry," I said, taking ahold of one of her hands again and squeezing it. "I'm so scared I can't think straight. I'm sorry for both of us."

We lapsed into silence, each lost in our own dreadful thoughts. I kept picturing different ways he might kill us one day.

Finally, she shrugged. “Sorry… I’d say forget it, but how can we? Unless you can somehow summon the cops, the FBI, the CIA and my dad and make this all go away.”

I shook my head. “I’m just so freaked out right now.”

She waved a listless hand. “That’ll pass once the hopelessness settles in.”

Then Cheryl began to laugh and cry at the same time, and I heard the beginning of hysteria in her voice. I certainly understood because I was trying to fight it off myself.

“Have you tried to escape?” I asked.

Her laughter became more high pitched. “That’s a great idea! I’ll have to write that down.” She looked expectantly around the empty room. “That is if I can find a pencil.”

I drew away from her. “You don’t have to be a bitch about it.”

She calmed down and threw me an apologetic look, then held up two fingers. “Twice actually. The first time I fought him. I went crazy. I scratched, bit, and then I tried to gouge his eyes out and he let go. I ran as fast as I could through the house. I was like a mad woman, screaming my head off. He caught up to me, though. That bought me my first night in that cage of his.”

She lapse into silence, shuddering at the memory, and the night I just spent in that same confined space returned to my mind with a vicious bite.

“And the second time?” I asked.

“We were in the kitchen. He forgot to put the cuffs on me, though in retrospect I doubt it, he thought I was thoroughly cowed by then. He was at the stove, his back to me. There were some pots in the drying rack, so I rushed over, grabbed the largest and whacked him in the head.”

I suddenly laughed in spite of myself. She looked at me and smiled wanly.

"I know," she said in response to my laughter. "Pretty cliché, right? But I didn't hit him hard enough. " Her face clouded and she looked away. "He beat me so bad I could hardly move for two days."

That chilled me. "God," I whispered.

"So now I'm too scared to try," she continued. "Which was the point of the beating, I guess."

I began to think frantically. I had to get out of there, and get Cheryl out, too. "We've got to escape," I said feverishly. "There has to be a way."

"It's not as easy as you'd think. He has this whole place rigged for his sick game."

"We have to try," I said fiercely.

She looked me in the eye then. "It's a lot less tempting when you remember that his dick isn't as dangerous as a bullet through the head."

My mouth fell open. I remembered him putting the gun against my temple and the thought deflated me a little.

"Do you know his name?" I asked.

"Daddy."

"No," I persisted. "His real name."

She shook her head. "No, just Daddy."

"That's so creepy," I said, then remembered my stupid HookedUp safe word — mommy. Ugh. I had no idea what I'd been thinking. Of course, I had to admit to myself I hadn't been thinking at all, or I wouldn't be in this awful mess.

"You want creepy? You should meet his half-brother. Daddy calls him 'Buddy-Boy.' It's like being in a locker room when they get together."

"A half-brother?" She nodded. I grabbed her arm with a sudden surge of hope. "So someone else knows he's keeping you here." Then I had a horrible thought. "He doesn't… has Buddy-Boy… ever…?"

She shook her head no. “Daddy doesn’t like to share. But Buddy-Boy’s not going to give Daddy’s secrets away, I can promise you. He’s just as bad, the bastard. Maybe even worse. When he looks at you it’s as if he doesn’t see you at all, he looks right through you, like you’re nothing. Like he could kill you without a second thought.”

I slumped, looking around the bare room. I looked at the shutters and wondered if I could try to pry one of the slats loose. However, they were metal and looked very solid.

“Why is he doing this?” I asked quietly.

“Some people are just sick.”

20

Detective Kennedy

Ms. Meade's story had me disturbed. I had a friend in a precinct in Baltimore who landed a case involving a HookedUp meet gone wrong. They found the missing woman eventually, or the pieces of her, rotting in a dumpster.

I've seen family or friends of missing people before, and they seem to naturally run to the worst case scenarios, but my intuition told me this might actually be one of those. Sometimes I got a feeling about a case, a tingling of the senses, and this was one of those. My gut almost never lets me down.

Lemuche didn't seem as concerned, though. I looked over at him. He was putting out an APB for Addison Clifton, giving her description, last known whereabouts and so on, but he was whistling while he did it. I could tell he thought Ms. Meade was a nervous type that was creating an unnecessary drama.

We had only been partners for a couple of weeks, and I still hadn't really made up my mind about him.

On the surface he seemed casual and even cautiously friendly, but I detected a reserved detachment in him. Maybe it was because he was younger than me and we had a generational difference in perspectives, or maybe our personalities didn't mesh, I didn't know.

The first day I met him I tried calling him by his first name, which is Eddy, but he quickly shut that down. He said he preferred for me to address him by his last name, Lemuche. Maybe it was a way of making sure our partnership stayed professional rather than personal. Or maybe it was just locker room type bullshit, like me and my buddies did back in high school. It rankled, though, because you needed to feel close to your partner, to trust them.

Regardless, I was stuck with him at the moment.

I went onto Addison Clifton's social media sites. She had a Facebook page, but it was set to privacy mode, only friends could see her posts, so that was a bust. She didn't do X or TikTok, but I found her on Instagram. There were some pictures of her and Ms. Meade, and one or two of Addison solo. I studied her face. She was pretty, certainly, but there was a haunted quality about her. I scrolled until I found some older posts. These showed a different Addison. She was with a man and a boy in these, and she almost glowed with contentment. It made me wonder.

Lemuche finished what he was doing and looked at me. "Should we try to get a warrant for HookedUp?" he asked.

I shook my head. "I don't think a judge'll give it until we have more evidence that she's in real danger." I sat back in my chair and regarded him. "Have you ever been on a dating site?" I knew he wasn't married.

He laughed. "Me? Nah. You?"

I shook my head. "Nope. I do it the old fashioned way and try to meet women in bars or at the gym." Or at work. I was currently seeing a woman who worked patrol, but I wasn't gonna share that with him. "I was just asking because I'm trying to figure out how these things work. Do they go to each other's homes, or do they meet up somewhere more neutral?"

He shrugged. "Both, I'd guess. Though this site advertises the rough stuff. Not sure I'd want a potential psycho coming to my place, or go to hers either."

I nodded. "That's what I was thinking. My bet's on a cheap motel somewhere."

"Makes sense."

"Okay," I said and stood up, picking my discarded jacket off the back of my chair. "Let's go check out her place, then case some motels in her area. I put a BOLO on her license plate, but until we get a hit, it's our best bet right now."

"Yeah, okay." Lemuche got out of his chair, grabbed his gun out of a drawer and fixed it to his belt holster. He put his own jacket on, then held out his hand. "I'll drive."

I tossed him the keys.

We found the key where Ms. Meade said we would and entered Addison's house, calling out her name in case she had returned, but there was no response. The house was small and minimally decorated.

Lemuche looked around, frowning. "Must be some kind of neat freak."

I nodded. It was scrupulously tidy.

We went through the place room by room, looking for anything that might lead to her current location, a discarded note, a receipt, things like that, but came up empty. I noted the laptop on the coffee table, but Ms. Meade had already told us it was password protected.

"Nothing here, " Lemuche said.

He was right. I pulled out my phone and pulled up several motels in the area. "Let's go," I said.

We hit pay dirt on the third motel.

The clerk, a skinny guy with two days beard growth and a receding hairline, looked at the picture of Addison that Lemuche held out to him.

"Yeah," he said immediately. "I recognize her. She came pretty often."

"Was she here with a man?" asked Lemuche.

The clerk shrugged. "Maybe, but I never saw nobody but her. She was the one that booked the rooms and paid for them. What she did after that's her business."

"How many nights did she typically stay?" I asked.

"Just one night."

I nodded. "When was the last time you saw her?"

He checked his computer. "Three nights ago."

That fit the time frame Meade said she went missing.

"Did you see her go?" Lemuche probed further.

The clerk shook his head. "Nope. Never did."

"Thanks," I said and we left.

It was actually Lemuche's idea to check the parking lot in case her car was still there.

It was. We found it parked near the last room she'd rented.

I went back to the clerk and asked him if the room she'd booked was vacant. He checked, said it was. I got the key and Lemuche and I checked it out. A maid had already been through so there was nothing to see. I left and headed around the building.

"Where're you going?" called Lemuche.

"Dumpster," I called back.

He joined me. It didn't take us long to discover some evidence. Under several bags of trash we spied a purse. I lifted it out using a pen. It wasn't clasped so Lemuche pulled it open and removed a wallet from the roomy interior. It belonged to Addison Clifton.

I turned to him. "I think we can get that warrant now."

21

Addison

Cheryl and I were separated again. He took her back to the room next to mine. I could hear him raping her, hear her whimpers and stifled screams, and I waited for my turn, which always came.

I wanted to fight, do anything to make him go away, but I was starting to become truly exhausted. The fear, dread and emotional turmoil was beginning to take its toll on me. I was becoming listless, like someone who'd given up. When he wasn't invading my body, there was nothing to do, just lie there, chained to the bedpost, staring at the slow march of time through the window's shutters.

At first, I used the time alone to plan ways to escape him, but I needed to be unshackled to make that happen, and he obviously wasn't going to do that. If I needed to use the bathroom, he unlocked the cuffs and firmly led me down the hall, waiting just outside until I was done, then drag me back to the room that was my private purgatory.

I often knocked on the wall that separated Cheryl and me, and sometimes she'd talk to me but other times I was met by total silence. I wondered if she was beginning to lose her mind; she'd been kept in that awful house longer than me. So I kept trying to engage her, but I could never tell what was really going on since I couldn't actually see her.

Since the chili he hadn't brought me into the kitchen again. He brought me sandwiches and water. I ate and drank because I knew if I didn't I'd never have the strength to escape. But I was beginning to wonder if I ever would. He was beating me down with each long drawn out moment.

I woke from sleep riddled with dark Stygian dreams to find Cheryl sitting on the bed next to me. She was softly stroking my hair. I struggled to sit up. My right arm was numb from the tightness of the handcuff.

"What time is it?" I asked, hoarsely.

She just shrugged.

"Where is he?" I asked, not liking the edge of fear creeping into my voice.

"I don't know."

"How long have you been in here?"

"Not long," she responded. "Maybe ten minutes or so."

My body was so stiff and sore I could barely move. I clutched the robe around me and leaned back against the wall.

"I don't know how long I can take this," I whispered.

She tilted her head and regarded me quietly for a moment. Then she said, "I don't know. You seem like a pretty strong woman. I think most would have cracked already."

"You haven't," I said.

She laughed dully. "You're wrong, I feel like I've given up. But you seem to still have some fight in you. I see it in your eyes, buried, yeah, but still there."

"I don't feel strong."

She flicked a stray strand of hair out of my eyes. "People in a crisis often find strength they didn't know they had."

I smiled grimly. Yeah, right. "You sound like a fortune cookie. Or a shrink."

"I'm a therapist," she said matter of factly.

I gaped at her. "What? You're kidding."

She shook her head sadly. "I specialize in helping teens with mental health issues."

I shook my head. "Wow." I don't know why that surprised me, but it did. Maybe I thought therapists would be older or stronger or something. Of course, most therapists don't get raped on a daily basis.

"You *have* to stay strong," she continued. "Daddy's dangerous. He's abusive and brutal, but he also enjoys playing with our minds."

That's when I realized that my lassitude was just what he had hoped to achieve. I was being submissive and not fighting back. He had cowed me with fear of retribution, or the wan hope of lulling him into a false sense of security in order to escape. I was doing exactly what he wanted.

I sat up straighter and felt a steely resolve take tentative roots inside. "He can take my body, but I'll never let him control my mind," I said firmly.

Cheryl sat back and studied the carpet. "You'd be surprised how easily some people allow themselves to be controlled. It was always one of the things that fascinated me the most in my study of psychology."

No! I wasn't going to let that be me. I shook my head fiercely. "That asshole's just a bully. Muscles and a gun are all he has going for him. I refuse to let him touch my mind."

She looked at me for a long moment, then nodded slightly and said, "Maybe you're right. But keep on your guard. It's the weapons you *can't* see that are the real danger."

We sat together for several hours, not saying much. What was there left to say? This situation really sucks? We already knew that. But it was comforting to have her near, to not feel so awfully alone.

The light finally disappeared and we were left in darkness. At some point we both must have drifted off because I was suddenly startled by the sound of the door being flung back against the wall. I sat up abruptly, disoriented. I felt Cheryl stir next to me.

He was standing in the open doorway.

"Dinner."

He took us into the kitchen one at a time. Cheryl went first, then he came back for me. I eyed him furiously as he unlocked my handcuff. He noted my expression but didn't react, just yanked me up and dragged me out of the room.

Cheryl was already cuffed by the ankle to the table when I entered. He went through the same routine with me then stood back rubbing his hands together and regarding us both with a big smile.

"You're both in for a treat tonight."

Cheryl and I looked at one another, and she looked frightened. I was worried his words had a deeper sinister meaning, and she would know, she'd had more experiences with him than me. I braced myself for the worst and looked back at him, trying not to let him see my fear.

He laughed again. "But I'll bet you can guess what it is already." He pointed to me. "You. What do you think it is?" he asked me.

"I have a name," I replied between my teeth.

The laughter in his face died. "That you do. So, Addison, can you guess what it is?"

"I'm putting my money on something sadistic." His eyes narrowed and he frowned. "But try slitting your own throat — that would be enough for me," I added, my voice dripping with venom.

He took one long step toward me and slapped me hard across the face. "Behave."

My cheek smarted and I felt tears sting my eyes.

He dismissed me then and turned to Cheryl. “You?”

I could see she was very nervous. “I don’t know,” she said quietly. “Something smells good, though.”

He beamed at her. “It doesn’t just smell good, it’s excellent. Chicken Provencal.” He looked from her to me. I was confused, and he immediately noted it. “You, my dear, are a lucky woman.”

I snorted with contempt. Yeah, I was lucky, alright. It wasn’t every woman that got beaten and raped every day. I wanted to punch his face so badly my palm itched, but I refrained from speaking.

“It’s an old recipe,” he continued, “But a cherished one in my family. You’ll love it, I promise.”

He turned from us and busied himself with dishing out the food. He set a sturdy plastic plate before me. I saw chicken, tomatoes and black olives in a light buttery wine sauce. The aroma made my stomach rumble. I was awfully tired of the dull parade of sandwiches, so despite my rediscovered rebellion, my mouth began to water.

He came back with a plate for himself and sat between us like the last time we were all together.

“Dig in, girls,” he said and began to eat.

Cheryl followed suit, picking up her plastic fork and taking a bite.

I sat there, staring at my plate like a stubborn, recalcitrant child refusing to eat her dinner. For one thing, I noted that unlike Cheryl I hadn’t been provided with a utensil.

He glanced at me and said, “What’s wrong? Don’t you like chicken?”

“No.”

Cheryl looked up from her plate and nodded her head very slightly, giving me a cautionary look.

“You should eat. It’s really quite delicious,” he prodded.

I shoved my plate away, but privately I was dying to gobble the whole thing up.

He gave me a hard look that promised retribution.

"Add-i-son," he said, drawing out my name sarcastically, "You should be more appreciative. It takes time and skill to prepare a great meal." He leaned in and narrowed his eyes to slits. "Eat."

I started to reach for the plate then stopped myself and raised my head, looking directly into those gray eyes with the little black specks. "You can't shove everything you want into me," I retorted.

A slow smile spread across his face. "Don't be too sure of that." Then he sat back and took another mouthful. "I hear starving is extremely unpleasant," he said without looking in my direction.

"So is being raped," I snapped back. I looked over at Cheryl for support.

"You should eat," she said quietly.

I was so surprised at her undermining me my mouth dropped open and I just gaped at her.

He jabbed his knife toward me and I involuntarily jerked back. "It's getting cold," was all he said though.

I slowly reached out my hand and pulled my plate back toward me. I looked from it to Cheryl. "Why don't I have a fork?" I asked.

"Forks are for good girls. Have you been a good girl?"

I grabbed up the chicken thigh and took a large bite, never taking my eyes from him, and began chewing. It really *was* delicious. The fucking bastard.

"Great, huh?" he asked, though I could see he didn't expect a reply. "It's my grandmother's recipe. Now there was a woman who knew how to cook! My mother's mother. She and my grandfather came to this country from France with fifty dollars in their pocket, and two years later she opened a restaurant. I started working there when I was just a small kid. I bussed tables, took out the garbage, mopped the floors, whatever. Then she let me help prep the food. I learned a lot, more than any stupid cooking school. Unfortunately, it didn't last long. She died too young and the restaurant closed."

He lapsed into thoughtful silence as he continued to eat.

If he thought I was going to thaw over his sweet little family story, if he thought I would begin to view him as more human, he was wrong.

"Is that what you do? You're a chef?" I asked. "When you're not abusing women, that is."

He didn't get offended. Maybe the two things were one and the same to him, a true psychopath.

"No," he responded matter of factly. "I could've been, but I went another way."

"I bet old grandma would be so proud," I retorted sarcastically.

His face darkened. "Finish your dinner."

22

Barb

It had been four days since Addy went missing. What the hell were the police doing? She was on my mind all the time, and I was beginning to fuck up at work. My boss, Peter, wanted to know what the hell was wrong with me. Seriously, dude? I mean it wasn't exactly a secret that my best friend — and one of our co-workers — was missing and presumed abducted. As far as I was concerned he could shove his marketing stats up his fat ass.

Unfortunately, I'm a bit of an open book when it comes to my feelings so he suggested I take a personal day. I suggested he fuck himself and took two. He didn't argue, he was used to me. Anyway, I think he wanted me out of the office, or at least a good distance away from him for a while. That was fine by me.

The next day the first thing I did was drive to the police station. I decided Kennedy or Lemuche had better have some damn answers.

"So what the hell have you two idiots been doing?" I demanded when I was led back to their desks. "Why haven't you found Addison yet?"

Lemuche raised his eyebrows in surprise, but it was Kennedy who answered me.

"We're working on it, Ms. Meade. Unfortunately, other than locating her abandoned car, we haven't found any solid leads. It's a big city, with lots of suburbs, and past that there's a lot of rural countryside and farm land. She could be anywhere. I promise you, we're diligently working on her case. Unfortunately, things like this can take time, more than any of us like."

Lemuche tapped his pen on the desk, giving me a look full of meaning. I knew what he was trying to tell me, he thought I was getting in the way, but I ignored him for the moment.

I felt my face grow hot. "You're presuming she *has* time. What if the maniac who took her decides to kill her?"

I regretted the words the second they popped out of my mouth. It was the first time I'd said aloud the thing I was most scared of. I had a sick feeling in my stomach. Horrified, I wondered if he'd already done it, if the guy who took her had already killed her. I suddenly wanted to cry.

Instead I twisted my fingers and asked, "What about that website. HookedUp? Were you able to find anything there?"

"Not yet," replied Kennedy. "We applied for a warrant but only got it yesterday. The administrators of the site haven't responded yet. I'm sorry, but we have our hands tied there."

"Why haven't they responded?" I demanded.

"I don't know. Typically these companies get back within twenty-four hours if it's an urgent criminal investigation. Unfortunately, they haven't. If we haven't heard from them by the end of the day we'll get a court order to force them to comply."

"Fuck that! Get a court order now!" I said, banging my fist on Lemuche's desk, and I could tell it pissed him off. Tough.

"Please calm down, Ms. Meade," said Kennedy.

"How can I calm down when Addy's still out there?"

"We'll find her."

I crossed my arms and gave him a greasy eye. "Oh, really? And how're you guys going to do that sitting here? Or do you expect the dickhead who took her to personally deliver her to you?"

Kennedy actually smiled a little. A very little.

"I promise you, we're working on it," he said.

I made a wry face and looked over at Lemuche. "Silence is golden when you can't think of a good answer, is that it, buddy?"

His eyes widened a moment, then his expression turned dark. He was about to make a hot retort when Kennedy quickly intervened.

"Ms. Meade, I appreciate you're upset, but Detective Lemuche and I are doing everything we can right now."

"Doesn't look like it from where I'm standing."

Kennedy got up from behind his desk, took me by the arm and began to lead me toward the door.

"Thank you for coming by, Ms. Meade, but you're correct, we can't do our jobs staying here talking to you. As I told you before, we'll keep you informed of anything we discover. Have a good day."

And with that he opened the door and gently but firmly pushed me out. I stood on the other side staring at the closed door fuming.

The fat deputy behind the front desk was watching me closely.

"Oh, go eat a bag of dicks," I growled at him and left the station. Outside I pulled out my phone and called Luke.

"So, are all cops stupid or just lazy?" I demanded when he answered.

He hung up.

23

Addison

The next morning was the beginning of just another day in hell. I heard him taking Cheryl in the next room and braced myself for my turn. He surprised me by bringing her to my room instead and then leaving, shutting us in.

She came over and slumped listlessly on the bed beside me. I took her hand.

"You okay?" I asked.

She let out a bitter little laugh. "What do you think?"

For once I wasn't handcuffed to the headboard, either he'd forgotten — which I doubted — or he decided I was tamed. I got off the bed and went to the window, gazing wistfully through the little shutter slits. All I could see was green lawn that was a bit overgrown.

"I hate feeling so helpless," I said quietly.

"I know," agreed Cheryl.

I grabbed one of the metal slats. "When he's inside of me…." I couldn't finish the thought, didn't even want the memory in my head.

She sighed. "At least he's quick."

"We have to get out of here somehow," I said, squeezing the slat so hard it hurt. "Maybe if we work together we can find a way." The edge bit into my fingers and a tiny trickle of blood peeped out from beneath one of them. "I'm tired of being scared, and I'm so damn tired in general."

"Trauma does that," she said. "But we can't give up."

She got up and came to stand beside me, putting an arm around my shoulders. "Like I said before, you're strong. Maybe that's why he chose you. You've stood up to him so far, so don't give up. Then he wins. Keep fighting."

"*You* don't fight," I replied, trying to keep from sounding bitter.

"I tried. I told you how it ended each time."

I looked her in the eye. "So, what? Now it's my turn to get punished?"

My response surprised her. She slowly shook her head. "Sorry. I didn't mean it like that. It's just… I want you to try and get out of here."

"You want out of here too, don't you?"

She removed her arm and sighed. "What do you think?"

She turned and sat back down on the bed. We both drifted with our own thoughts for a few silent minutes. I thought about the men I'd been with through HookedUp and shuddered. So, so stupid. I thought those trysts would take me out of myself, numb my pain, instead it brought on so much more. I kept wanting to blame myself, and I certainly carried my share, but I reminded myself over and over that he was the one who was to blame, not me. He did this. And not just to me, but to Cheryl too.

"I used to like men," I said softly. "And sex." I laughed bitterly. "But after this I doubt I'll be able to stand either anymore."

"This isn't about sex, Addison," said Cheryl in a tired but firm voice. "It's about control."

I wondered if we were the first women he'd abducted, or if we were merely the last in a line of them. That thought brought me up fast. I swung around and looked at her.

"What if he's done this before?" I asked.

"What?"

"What if we aren't the first women he's held captive, Cheryl?"

She didn't answer.

"Because…," I stopped and looked outside again. A chill tripped up my spine. "If there's been others, what happened to them? He wouldn't have just gotten tired of them and let them go, would he? He would've killed them."

A strange look appeared on her face, and she stared at me open-mouthed, but I could tell this idea wasn't new to her.

I grabbed the slat again and yanked as hard as I could, but of course it was solidly welded together and bolted into the wall. "We have to get out of here," I whispered.

She was silent a moment, then asked in a voice so soft I barely heard her, "How?"

"I don't know."

Cheryl was silent for a moment, then said, "Until we can figure out a way, we need to make sure he doesn't get tired of us so we don't end up in a shallow grave somewhere."

I swung on her. "Are you serious?"

"Deadly serious. I don't want to die here."

"So what are you suggesting?" I asked. "Act like we're enjoying sex with him? Act like we actually like his company? I'm not that good of an actress, Cheryl. Every time he comes near me I want to vomit."

“I know. But it’s survival now, Addison. What choice do we have?”

I shook my head vigorously. “Never. I can’t.”

24

Addison

The door was flung open and he stood there grinning at us. Smiling, like we were all one happy trio, just another normal day. He looked straight at me and I pushed myself back against the shutters.

"Bathroom?" he asked.

I glanced quickly at Cheryl, who nodded, then said, "Yes."

He walked over, took firm hold of my arm and dragged me out of the room to the bathroom. I hated myself for being grateful, but I had to pee desperately. I went in, quickly shutting the door behind me and did my business. Feeling relieved again, I turned on the faucet and began washing my hands. I eyed the bathtub and ardently wished I could take a bath. I hadn't washed in days and felt filthy.

He called me from the other side of the door. "Time's up. Let's go."

"I'm almost done," I called back.

The door flew open. “Let’s go,” he said gruffly.

I turned off the water and dried my hands. He stepped forward and yanked the towel away. “Enjoying Cheryl’s company?” he asked.

I remembered her advice about giving him no reason to do away with us, but I couldn’t help myself. I raised my chin and replied, “Not as much as you are.”

That made him smile again. “We do get loud, don’t we? Maybe I’ll let you watch sometime.”

The thought made me gag.

“No, thank you,” I said. My eyes slid from his face to the gun in his belt, then quickly back up again. “The only thing I want to watch is you being led away in handcuffs or dying. I prefer the last one.”

I knew what I was about to do was really risky, but I was feeling desperate. I quickly lunged forward, grabbed the handle of the gun and jerked it out of his pants. I immediately took a step back and tried to aim it at him, but I wasn’t fast enough.

He was a blur as he launched at me, seizing my wrist in a painful vise-like grip, twisting it viciously. I kicked his shins as hard as I could but he just squeezed harder. I screamed from the pain and the gun dropped from my hand.

Still clamped onto my wrist, he quickly leaned down and retrieved the gun. He replaced it in his belt at his back. He never took his eyes off my face, which now had tears of pain wetting it. He moved toward me until his face was an inch away from my own.

“It’s time for another lesson.”

Cheryl was sitting cuffed to the table again when he dragged me into the kitchen. He slammed me into the chair opposite her and cuffed my own ankle. Then he stepped back and looked at each of us in turn.

“Tea anyone?”

My wrist was reddened and stinging. I made a face at him. "Fuck you," I replied.

I didn't look at Cheryl because I knew she was probably giving me another one of her warning looks. I didn't want to put her in danger, but I felt like I was barely hanging on. I wanted to scream at him, at the world, at God or fate for landing me there in that horrible house.

"I'll have some," said Cheryl quietly.

I watched him pour her a cup from a steaming kettle and sit it in front of her. "Careful," he said. "It's hot."

He returned to the stove, poured another cup and sat down between us. He blew on the tea then took a small sip. "Really hot."

He sat his cup down and got up again. He went to one of the cupboards and took down a large jar of honey. He brought it back to the table, unscrewed the cap and set it next to his steaming cup.

"Honey is amazing stuff," he said casually. "We love it, but when you think about it, honey is actually pretty gross. Bees drink the nectar of flowers then regurgitate it back in their comb. So we're eating bee vomit. And we've been doing it for centuries. People actually hunted for it as long as eight thousand years ago. It was their most prized food."

He rose to his feet again in one swift movement and reached out for me, yanking me to my feet. I was so surprised I didn't even fight him. He slammed me down across the table and raised my robe up almost to my shoulders. Oh, shit, I thought. Time for another rape. And this time Cheryl has to watch. I tried to buck against him, but he held me firmly down by grabbing one of my arms and twisting it up behind me. Pain shot through my arm and shoulder.

He began to softly stroke the curve of my back. I turned my head toward Cheryl, who was nervously looking from me to him. I heard some heavy staccato panting and realized it was coming from me.

"Let me go," I pleaded with him. "Please."

He didn't answer at first, just continued his stroking, then finally he said, "They found the remains of honey in pots in a tomb they dated to over five thousand years ago." His hand glided down one of my thighs, caressing it gently. "And did you know the ancient Egyptians used honey in their embalming process?" He leaned down and whispered near my ear. "But you know what's really cool? Honey also has medicinal uses."

I saw his free hand reach for his cup of tea. Instantly I knew what was coming and started to struggle. He only tightened his grip on my twisted arm. He poured the scalding tea onto my lower back.

Cheryl cried out at the same time a howl like a wounded animal was torn from my lungs. The pain was so incredibly intense, like being branded with a red hot poker. I was in hellish agony. The initial shock of heat was quickly replaced by an unending, searing ache, and I thought I could smell the faint, sickening odor of burnt skin filling the air.

Tears blurred my vision and somewhere I could hear him softly shushing my whimpers.

"Now, now," he said. "I told you honey had medicinal uses. It even can be used to help soothe burns."

Through the tears I saw him dip two fingers into the jar, then felt him smearing honey on the wound. He released my arm but I didn't rise up; I could only remain sprawled across the table choking on the sobs my chest pushed out.

25

Cheryl

The primary reason for torture is often far more than inflicting pain on a person. No, the aim is to destroy the person's sense of self and control. They want them to feel helpless and dependent on the person torturing them. They want to humiliate and degrade them.

When I was studying psychology I came across something called the "three D's," developed by a psychiatrist, Albert Biderman. They are Debility, causing mental and physical exhaustion; Dependency, creating total dependance; and Dread, instilling intense fear.

For us it began with the forced nudity and the sexual assaults, meant to instill shame and destroy our self-worth, and the constant attacks will exhaust you and really wear down your will to fight back.

Next, Daddy holds all the keys for us to be sustained, he can give us food and water or withhold them, making us forced to rely heavily on him.

And the dread… I think that's fairly obvious. When you've been hit or beaten enough times — or are scalded with boiling water — you learn that feeling fast.

I watched him burn her back and instantly knew poor Addison would have a horrible time recovering from that. Oh, the burn would heal, though there would likely be scarring, but it was the mental wounds that wouldn't be so easy to get over. Women who survive captivity — assuming she would — experience a form of PTSD, and I suspected she'd be a long-time victim of nightmares, severe anxiety, paranoia and emotional avoidance in the future, things very difficult to overcome.

Of course I was forced to witness the whole thing. Many people witnessing torture of others feel intense guilt and trauma, and even though I was aware of this it was still a hard thing to watch, and despite knowing better, I felt guilty. Mostly that I was relieved it happened to her and not me. Not nice, I know, but fear sometimes strips you of your empathy.

Daddy knew the psychology of torture well, and he was systematically trying to dismantle Addison's sense of identity and steal our humanity. In short, to completely break us.

I had begun to believe Addison's strong will might escape all that, but after what just happened I wasn't so sure anymore. That was enough to break anyone. She was sobbing uncontrollably when he led her out of the kitchen. I didn't get a very good look at her wounds, but I hoped Daddy would at least treat them with something or bandage it. I wasn't putting a lot of hope in that, though.

And me? I'm sorry to say so, but I think I had long ago given up on myself. Maybe it was loss of self-esteem, or maybe it was boredom and a sense of no purpose in my life. But whatever it was, that's why I was such an easy target for him in the first place. He knew he'd easily lure me and he did, and now I was his prisoner.

26

Daddy

Addison really had such a lovely body it was a shame to burn it that way, but she had to be taught a lesson. I wasn't about to let her keep rebelling, so she had to be tamed. I enjoy the fight but there is a limit to what I'll put up with.

It shocked me when she went for my gun like that. Things could have really gotten out of control. I would've hated to have gotten rid of her, because I was enjoying her. Still… if she didn't start behaving things would have to change. That would be too bad.

After the honey lesson I put Addison back in her room without Cheryl. She needed time alone to consider her position here. I was pretty confident the scalding had her subdued. When I left the room she was curled up on the bed in a fetal position, quietly crying. That was good. It meant she was calming down.

I would go back in later and check the burn. It wasn't the first time I'd done something like that to someone and so was sure it would heal fine. Maybe I would even bandage it or something, I'd have to wait and see. She would probably have a scar, but scars were sexy.

I headed for my computer to get some work done when my phone rang. It was my half-brother.

"Hey, Buddy-Boy, what's up?" I greeted him.

"I can only talk a minute," he said. "Still working, just stepped out a moment. Dwayne's been calling me. I haven't answered any of his calls, but he's being persistent. Know what he's up to this time?"

Dwayne had fathered Buddy-boy by another women, and when she took off he came to live with us. Poor bastard. And for as long as I could remember Buddy-boy refused to call him *Dad*. I hated the old asshole myself, so I understood.

"Yeah, he was here a few days ago. The same old shit, he wanted money. He's probably already blown it and is trying to tap you. Don't give him any."

He guffawed. "As if I would. I'm surprised he's even trying, the shitbag. Thanks for the heads up."

"Why don't you block him on your phone? I have."

"Cuz then he'd show up at my place like he did yours, and I sure as shit don't want that."

"You're hardly ever home anyway," I said, "So I wouldn't worry about it."

"I gotta go back in. Talk to you later."

He hung up and I got in a good four hours of work.

That's the great thing about being a freelance programmer, I can work at home and be on my own schedule. My off time is my own, and I can go about the business I really enjoy without any interference. I shut off the laptop, stood and stretched. I wanted a beer, but I decided to check in on Addison first.

She was still curled up on the bed, facing the wall, when I entered. She looked like she was sleeping. I lifted the robe and investigated the burn spot. The skin was red, blistered and swollen, and there was a bit of liquid oozing at one spot. I was suddenly aware that she had awoken, she'd abruptly become too still, too tense. I said nothing.

I left the room and went into my bathroom to get the can of burn relief spray and a bandage. I kept the spray for occasional kitchen burns. When I returned she was in the same position I'd left her, but I could tell she was alert.

I treated her wound, bandaged it and left, locking the door firmly behind me.

In the kitchen I opened a beer and considered what to prepare for dinner. I opted for salmon, smashed mini potatoes and green beans. I checked and decided I had enough to invite the girls in to dinner. Though Addison brought on her punishment herself, a good meal might make her feel better, especially with a nice bottle of Sauvignon Blanc. I wasn't a nice guy, but I wasn't a total dickhead either.

I pulled out the ingredients and began to whistle while I started the prep.

The day had begun badly, but I had successfully turned things around, as usual. It was going to be a nice evening after all.

27

Addison

I pulled the bandage off and felt along my lower back, letting my fingers brush the remnant of his latest assault. The blisters rose like small, obscene little mountains beneath them, an echo of the brutal encounter I'd had with the boiling liquid. It would leave a scar, and I knew I'd always feel a phantom heat there. But it wasn't just the boiling tea, everything that had happened to me here would leave a lasting scar, a dark place inside seething with a tornado of fury, pain and remorse for my stupidity. I doubted a lifetime of therapy would ever erase it.

Assuming I had much of a future left.

I wondered if I was right and we weren't the first or the last women to be kept there. My mind conjured a desolate landscape full of shallow graves containing abruptly severed lives. Would we be next? If he could do what he had just done, it wasn't that big of a step to end my life or hers. I had to be careful, but I had to find a way out of this hell. I wasn't going to help him dig my grave. I had to find a way!

The light was fading when I heard the door behind me open again.

"Addison." It wasn't a question, he knew I was awake.

I refused to answer.

"Get up," he commanded.

I refused to move.

I could hear him cross the room in two quick strides. He grabbed my arm and jerked me upright. He looked through my wildly tousled hair into my eyes.

"Rule number three — when I ask you to do something, you do it. Now. Get up."

He released my arm and took a step back. I slowly rose to my feet, my mouth a thin line of hate, never taking my eyes off his.

"See? That wasn't hard. Let's go."

He pushed me ahead of him and I stumbled a bit, wondering what kind of torture I was walking into next.

When I entered the kitchen again I tried not to shudder, letting my eyes dart everywhere to see if he had another boiling kettle on. There were several covered pans on the stove but that was it. I looked to see if there was a knife anywhere, but no such luck.

Cheryl was already there, cuffed in her usual way and in her usual chair. Her eyes searched mine intently.

He sat me down and cuffed my ankle to the table then wandered over to the stove. He called over his shoulder, "Hungry, girls?"

It was amazing to me that he could act so casually after all the awful things he'd done to us, like we were merely house guests or something. At times I wondered if all this was a horrible, bizarre product of my mind, a nightmare I created for some crazy reason, and that none of it was real at all. It kept switching back and forth between a weird normalcy and a brutal hell, and I never felt prepared for either.

"Do you like salmon?" he asked, confirming the unreality of it all to me. Like he was just a normal, mannered dinner host.

The meal was a blur. I ate on auto pilot, shoving one small bite after another into my mouth with my fingers. He even served us wine, but I was so bemused I couldn't tell if it was any good or not. I drank very little of it.

When we finished he cleared the plates away and came to stand behind me. He placed his hands on my shoulders and I flinched. He leaned down until his lips were almost touching my ear. I cringed.

"You know something, Addison?" he said very softly. He paused a moment then said, "You're rank."

I actually turned and looked at him I was so surprised. Though probably true, it was the last thing I thought he'd say.

He moved away and uncuffed Cheryl. She stood close by while he did the same to me. "Let's go."

Taking each of us by the arm, he marched us out of the kitchen, down the hall and into the bathroom.

"Get in," he demanded, looking straight at me.

I looked around; I had no idea what he meant. "Get in — where?" I stammered.

He nodded to the bathtub. Shit. What disgusting, horrible thing was he about to do? He extended his arm and gave me a little push, sending me falling to the edge of the tub. "Get in."

I did as he asked, feeling so weird sitting in a robe in the empty tub. I watched while he attached Cheryl's ankle cuff to the toilet pipe, then he turned and looked down at me.

"Give me the robe."

Oh, shit.

"Do it," he continued through closed teeth.

Hesitantly I did so, feeling more naked and vulnerable than I ever had in my life. Was this it? I wondered. Had he put me there to make clean up easier after he killed me? An unbidden image of my lifeless body in the blood spattered tub rose in my mind. I began to tremble violently, suddenly scared out of my mind.

He reached down and I flinched backward. But his hand went to the stopper instead of me, he pressed it then turned on the faucet. Cold water rushed out, splashing my feet and legs. It soon turned warm, but as it rose above my waist I gasped. The warm water inflamed the blisters on my back, sending little waves of agony through me.

Then one of the most humiliating things I'd suffered so far occurred. He produced a bar of soap from a pocket, sat on the edge of the tub and… he began to wash me.

I don't know why, I couldn't process the reason, but being bathed like a child was in a way more shaming than anything else he'd done to me. I was so mortified. I think maybe it was the absolute control over me, how helpless I was at his hands, that so thoroughly demoralized me at that moment. I couldn't even look at Cheryl I was so embarrassed.

He scrubbed my body then began to wash my hair. I knew it was going to look lifeless and feel like straw after being cleansed with a bar of soap. He rinsed me thoroughly then he pushed down the stopper; I watched dully as the soapy water began to slowly drain. I wished it would carry me with it, let me disappear down the pipes. Being stuck in a shit filled sewer would be better that this.

28

Addison

I was beginning to feel exhausted. Even my mind began to dull, instead of dreaming up ways to escape or kill him, I found myself sitting for an hour or two on end, then suddenly realize I'd had no real coherent thought at all. Cheryl called this avoidance.

I'd read about PTSD once, and actively avoiding your own thoughts and difficulty concentrating was one of the symptoms. I tried to remember the other things people who'd been in captivity experienced. Distressing dreams. Check, I'd already had plenty of those. Easily startled. Check. Fear, shame and feeling isolated. Yep. However, there was one I would *never* allow myself to suffer from — Stockholm Syndrome.

I would never, ever let myself develop an emotional bond with that bastard. Never. But… sometimes I wondered about Cheryl. She seemed so meek with him, and did so little to resist him, even with her attitude.

I know he'd beaten her badly, and I could understand that fear, but she never even talked back to him. I reminded myself she had been kept by him for a longer time then me. So was it really a stretch to think maybe she was beginning to sympathize with him? She did routinely call him 'Daddy,' something I still refused to do, even in my mind.

I shook my head. That's where I'd sunk to.

I felt so debased and alone that I was accusing her of having Stockholm Syndrome, a poor woman who was in the same horrible situation I was in. She was the only thing keeping me sane. I suspected she felt the same about me. She and I were like men who fought together in battles, there was a closeness being forged between us.

And I didn't doubt for one second that we were in a battle. At the moment he was winning, but I'd seize any opportunity I could to reverse that tide. Despite the lassitude I was feeling at the moment, that thought was the only thing keeping me going.

However, he was keeping us in our separate rooms today.

So when he brought us together at the table later and announced he was treating us to a Saturday brunch, I was surprised. I tried to access the calendar in my head but I couldn't do it. I thought I'd been a captive for five days, but it might've been seven or ten, I couldn't tell anymore.

We were in the middle of crepes and fruit when there was a sudden knock on the back kitchen door.

He froze, startled.

It was my moment and I grabbed it.

"Help!" I screamed at the top of my lungs.

In a flash he was behind me, his hand clamped painfully over my mouth, whipping the gun from his pants and pressing into my neck.

From behind me he issued a fierce whispered warning to Cheryl, "One word and I'll kill you both."

My hearting was thumping against my chest. Please, I begged silently to whoever was on the other side of the door. *Please help us.*

"Who is it?" he called to the door in a normal voice.

"Got a package for you," a man replied, his voice muffled by the door.

"Leave it, I'll get it later."

"Can't," the stranger called back. "It's certified. I need a signature."

I chose that moment to bite into his hand. I bit so hard I felt blood.

He yelped and removed it from my mouth.

"Help!" I screamed. "We've been kidnapped!"

There was an explosion behind my eyes. He brought his hand down again on my temple with deadly force and my vision began to blur. I slumped over and fell to the floor, half unconscious. The room seemed to be spinning.

I heard quick footsteps and a door opening.

"Sign here," I heard the delivery man say.

I tried to call out again but the only thing to escape my lips was a feeble croak.

"Everything okay in there?"

I heard a chuckle. "Yeah, just the tv."

"Have a nice—" began the delivery guy but he was shut off by the door slamming in his face.

A small package was tossed onto the chair I'd fallen from, but it didn't fully land and fell to the floor beside me.

I heard more footsteps as I tried to take a deep breath and clear my vision.

"Very good girl," he said, I assumed to Cheryl.

With a herculean effort I opened my eyes and forced them to focus again. I pulled myself up a few inches and read the address on the package. It was addressed to M. Jondo, 1906 Wright Rd., Trouville....

A vicious kick sent me back.

When I looked up again he was standing over me, his face full of controlled fury.

"You, on the other hand...."

He unlocked my ankle cuff and began dragging me to the basement door. But all I could think of was the name and address — especially the address — I had seen. I did all I could to commit it to memory.

Maybe the tide was finally about to turn.

29

Barb

The day after my visit to the detectives' office I called Kennedy again and he gave me bad news.

"I don't make a practice of this," he sighed. I knew he thought I was being a pest and getting in the way of his investigation, but at least he hadn't hung up on me. "Can I have your assurance this conversation will remain between us?"

"Of course!" I assured him.

He resumed. "HookedUp sent us Ms. Clifton's profile along with the profiles of the men she messaged to meet."

"Finally!" I cried, feeling like a heavy pressure was lifted from my chest. "Now you can go make the one who took her tell you where she is!"

"Yes, we intend to *question* the men in the profiles, but —"

"So what the hell are you doing on the phone with me? Go get the bastard."

"Detective Lemuche and I are going to, Ms. Meade. The only problem is the last man she messaged back and forth with seems to be untraceable. He was the last one to have contact with her. They messaged back and forth two separate times, and then everything stopped."

I pulled the phone away and stared at it a moment, unsure I'd heard right, then put it back to my ear. "What do you mean, *untraceable*?"

"I mean there isn't a digital footprint of him."

"So, what?" I asked, frustrated and getting angry. "Like he used a burner phone or something? He's still had to have set up a profile, right? Can you even do shit like that with a burner?"

"Unfortunately, there are many ways to do it. It appears whoever met with her last has some technical savvy, or knows someone who does. So I'll be honest, here's the main reason I'm giving you this information at all… please think, Ms. Meade, did Ms. Clifton ever mention any of these guys' names to you? Especially the last one."

"No," I replied. "I didn't even know she was using this site until very recently. I already told you that."

He was silent a moment. "That's unfortunate," he finally said.

"Well, fuck a duck!" I snapped. "Is there any way to find this asshole? I mean, there's lots of devious, smart little techies out there, couldn't you get someone to find this bastard?"

"We're working on it."

"You always say that!" I groused, feeling exasperated and let down.

We hung up and I was so frustrated I wanted to kick something. However, I was in a liquor store so that would've been a bad idea.

30

Detective Kennedy

Lemuche and I began checking out the list of men Addison had meetings with on HookedUp. Excluding our mystery guy, there were five of them. We tracked down their home addresses and places of work.

Not surprisingly none of them were happy to see us.

To a man, they spent far too much time trying to convince us they didn't usually do that kind of site, and that they were really good guys (especially the two that were married).

At one point Lemuche got kind of rough with a guy named Tom. It wasn't anything physical, but he leaned on him a bit hard, and I could see the man literally start to sweat. You could see he was terrified we'd haul him off to jail any minute.

We checked their stories regarding their whereabouts since parting with Addison, and for the most part they checked out. They continued with their normal routines, and had people who vouched that their recent behavior wasn't unusual or out of the ordinary. If one of them was keeping her captive somewhere they would have to go to her occasionally, which would force them to explain unusual absences. Also, there was no appearance of scratches or evidence of any kind of physical altercation apparent on any of them, and in my experience most women put up some kind of fight if they are being taken somewhere by force.

Every one of them agreed to let us take a cheek swab to collect a DNA sample, which gave the appearance of their having nothing to worry about, though appearances can be misleading. The samples would go on file until we located her — or her body.

In other words, we were no farther along than before we talked to them.

I wasn't really surprised. Each had an open and upfront profile on the site, unlike the last man Addison met with. He was the one that held my interest.

We had someone in CCU working on discovering his true identity, but until he came up with anything there wasn't much me or Lemuche could do about our mystery man.

Lemuche was driving. I looked over and saw he was looking put out. Like I said, we hadn't been partners long, but I already discovered he didn't have much in the way of patience. If he didn't solve a case immediately he took it as a personal affront to his abilities as a detective.

"What's wrong?" I asked him.

He drummed his fingers on the steering wheel. "You'd think we would've found *something* by now. It's been five days since she went missing."

"We found her car," I replied mildly.

"That's not what I mean."

"Lemuche, detective work can take time and be frustrating, especially a missing person case, you know that."

He stared out the window for a moment then finally said, “What kind of woman does that anyway?”

“What?”

“Goes on to sites like that, the rough stuff, I mean. Was she a masochist, just another whore, or a needy woman looking for attention? Shit like that never leads to any good. Never. Stupid bitch.”

I looked at him, surprised at his attitude.

It made me wonder about his private life, which he never talked about. Maybe he’d had a bad experience with a woman in his past. There was something in his voice, an angry distain, that made me think so. It made me a little uncomfortable, and not for the first time I wished we hadn’t been assigned together, but we had a job to do so I put it out of my mind for the present.

“I don’t know,” I said slowly. “But, regardless of her motives, she didn’t deserve to be kidnapped. She certainly doesn’t deserve to lose her life.”

He glanced over at me, frowned a moment, then gave me a sheepish smile. “Yeah, you’re right. I just… I just don’t get people sometimes.”

“Who does?” I shrugged. “But we don’t have to understand them to give them justice, right?”

“Yeah.”

I glanced at the display on the dashboard, it was one-thirty in the afternoon. “Let’s take a break and grab some lunch. I know a place.”

Twenty minutes later we were sitting in a greasy little dive I frequent. The décor was shabby, the clientele shabbier, but the burgers were outstanding and didn’t cost much. Cheap beer, too, but since we were still on duty we ordered sodas. Lemuche opted for a salad over a burger. He was really fit, and looked like he did a lot of weight lifting, so whenever we were on shift he always went for the healthiest menu item he could find. No cop and donut cliche about him, that was for certain. Still, this place wasn't famous for making salads, and his looked sad and a little wilted.

I studied him over my burger. He was one of those guys who were way too uptight all the time. His muscular physique only added to the sense of controlled danger in him. Of course, that didn't hurt him in our line of work; more than one suspect got nervous around him, which sometimes benefitted us, and since I was older, it made playing good cop, bad cop easier. I could pass as the calm, mature one keeping the younger officer on a leash. Actually, once in a while that felt like the truth.

"So where do we look next?" he asked, wiping salad dressing off his chin with a paper napkin.

Good question.

I didn't have his impatience, but understood urgency in a missing persons case, and I felt like time was ticking away, and that if we didn't locate Addison soon it might be too late.

If only we had something, anything, that could lead to her trail and ultimately the person who had taken her.

31

Addison

I was back in the dog cage. After he got rid of the mail carrier he punched me in the face, then dragged me down the basement stairs, yanked off my robe and threw me in. I could have screamed when I heard the lock snap shut, but I refused to give him the satisfaction. I waited until he mounted the steps and shut the door, then yelled into my hands, venting all my fear and frustration into them.

I was in there for hours, and because the cage forced me into a crouched sitting position I was beginning to cramp up in places. I was cold, too. The basement was damp and chilly. I rubbed my arms and legs but it didn't help. I was also beginning to be hungry and really thirsty as well.

When the first sliver of moonlight struggled through the dusty window high on the wall, piercing the darkness with its eerie pinprick glow, I thought I'd scream. Would this nightmare never end? I watched it inch its way across the floor for what felt like an eternity before sleep mercifully overcame me.

It was daylight when he finally released me.

He bent down and fixed me with his eye. I gave him a blank look. His face suddenly crinkled.

"God, you stink!" he said, pulling away.

Of course I did. I had no access to a bathroom and had to relieve myself inside the cage, and I was sitting in my own filth.

He undid the padlock and swung the door open. I crawled out, covered in waste, my cramped muscles screaming in protest. It couldn't get any more humiliating. He marched me upstairs and right into the bathroom.

Thanks to my disgusting state, I was allowed to bathe myself. I hated myself for being grateful to him for it. The thought of his touch was horrific to me at that point. As the bath water was running, I went to the sink and drank straight from the tap I was so thirsty.

I was tempted to linger in the tub but he stood in the doorway, watching me the entire time, so I hastily scrubbed my body and washed my hair. He pulled the towel from the rack and held it out to me as a signal I should be done after that.

As I dried myself he disappeared, but only for a quick moment, then returned carrying my robe. I snatched it from him and wrapped myself in it, tying it tightly.

I was escorted back to my room. A plastic bottle of water and a sandwich was waiting for me. I wanted to leap on them but I just stood there, watching him warily. He hovered in the doorway, a small smile playing on his lips.

"I hope that taught you a lesson," he said, then closed the door.

Only after I heard the lock engage did I pounce on the food. It was tuna, which I've never cared for, but it could've been boiled slugs for all I cared, I was so hungry.

I had just finished eating when the door opened again and Cheryl was thrust into the room. He closed the door again immediately.

"Were you sent in to teach me the rules of behavior?" I asked angrily.

Her mouth opened in surprise. "What?"

I got up and began to pace the room, shooting her a furious glance now and then. She'd been so malleable and timid around him all this time I wanted to strangle her. I had not seen her try to stand up to him, not once. And when our first real chance of escape appeared she did absolutely NOTHING. She knew I was angry, and she began twisting the fabric of her robe between her fingers nervously.

"Did he…?" she began then stopped herself.

"What?" I snapped. "Throw some more boiling water on me?"

Her eyes opened wide and she gasped.

I waved her away. "No, he didn't."

"How bad *is* the burn?" she asked uneasily. "I haven't had a chance to see it. Does it still hurt? Do you want me to look at it for you?"

"What the hell's wrong with you?" I growled at her.

"What do you mean?"

"Why didn't you *do* something?" I almost screamed at her.

"I don't know what you're talking about," she replied defensively, taking a step back from me.

"That mail guy — why the hell didn't you scream? It would have been a lot harder for him to lie and wave it away if we had both yelled our lungs off. He couldn't pretend it was the tv then. You could've have screamed we were being held against our will, or that the house was on fire — something, for god's sake! Even if he couldn't have gotten inside, it would have been enough to make the guy suspicious and call the police. We had one chance — one! We could have finally escaped this nightmare, but you didn't do ANYTHING. You just sat there like you'd been muzzled." I walked up and got right in her face. "Do you like this? Have you finally become one of those sad women who start to like their kidnappers?"

She shook her head violent. “No. No, I was —” She stopped speaking abruptly and took another step away from me, then she dropped her head in her hands and began to cry.

“You were what?” I asked dangerously.

“I was scared,” she whispered so softly I barely heard her.

I refused to let myself soften or feel sorry for her. “As opposed to what? I’m scared all the damned time!” I searched her face a moment, trying to figure her out. “Don’t you want out of here, Cheryl?” I asked in a calmer tone.

“Stop asking me that!” she cried sharply.

“You gave me this whole pep talk about how I needed to stay strong so we could escape, then when the chance came, you — did – nothing! Instead of giving advice why don’t you grow a pair of balls!”

She balled her hands into fists. “There’s not a whole hell of a lot I can do when I’m chained to a fucking table!” she spat back at me.

“Your mouth wasn’t chained!” I yelled back.

Suddenly I felt all the fury drain from me, and I was suddenly exhausted. I went over to the shutters and dropped my head against them, feeling defeated.

“At least I tried,” I said softly.

I heard her begin to sob again but I didn’t raise my head. I listened as she walked over and sunk down on the bed.

“I just got…,” she began in a small voice, “I don’t know… it was like I was suddenly paralyzed or something. Like in those nightmares when you try to scream, but your throat closes up and nothing comes out.”

“You’re a therapist. How could you let fear get in the way of doing something to save yourself?” I asked dully.

She didn’t answer so I raised my head. She was looking steadily at me.

“I’m a therapist, yes,” she said, then added quietly, “But I’m also human, Addison. I’m not in a safe session with a patient. I’m not dealing with someone else's nightmares. I'm in one of my own. Fear can paralyze anyone if it's great enough."

I sighed and went over, sitting next to her on the bed. I leaned back against the wall and immediately winced at the sting from my unhealed back.

"Let me see," she said.

I waved her away. "Don't bother." Then I let out a harsh laugh. "Nothing you can do about it anyway."

"I'm so sorry, Addison," she whispered.

"Me, too." Then I looked over at her and smiled a little. "I'll tell you one thing, though. Yesterday wasn't a total wash."

"What do you mean?"

"I got a good look at the package."

She just stared back a moment then her face lit up. "You know his name!"

I shook my head. "Only his last name. Jondo."

"Jondo," she repeated, staring across the room, thinking. "I don't recognize it."

"No reason we should. But here's the thing, Cheryl — I know where we are. I know his street address."

Her face lit up, but then it clouded again.

"What's wrong?" I asked.

"He has to know you saw it."

"So?"

She looked me in the eye. "So, you just made yourself very dangerous to him."

32

Daddy

I sat at my desk, but I wasn't working. I just stared at the screen thinking hard about Addison. I liked this one, she was beautiful and brought enough fight to make things interesting. The ones that broke easily were always such a disappointment, they got boring fast. It was hard to find a perfect candidate, but it seems like I had one at last.

Only one problem, though. Addison was stubborn, and I had a feeling she wouldn't give up easily. That could become a problem if I didn't do something. She saw my name and address, which meant if she ever succeeded in getting away she'd bring me out into the open. Not good. I had an ally, but he might not be enough if things got out of hand.

That meant one of two things: I had to completely ensure she stayed secure here until I was done with her, or I would have to end things before I wanted to. I didn't like that last, but I might not have much choice in the end.

While I was weighing my options I heard a car pull up outside. I got up and looked through the blinds and groaned. What the fuck was he doing back so soon?

Before I could get to the front door and lock it, it opened. My father was standing there. He was a lot faster than his appearance would lead you to think.

"Aren't ya gonna ask me in?" he wanted to know.

"No. Get out," I said, "I'm working."

"So take a break," he said. "Isn't that one of those, whatchacallit – perks -- of being your own boss?"

"Dad, I'm busy, go away."

"You never seem to want to see me," he whined.

"Wonder why?" I asked wryly.

He pretended to be affronted, but he damned well knew I hated him, and he knew why. Or thought he did anyway.

"You can give me ten minutes," he said.

"Dad, I know you don't have the first concept about work, you've never held a job in your life, but —"

"Hey!" he interrupted in a huff, "I suffered from PTSD. That wasn't my fault."

"Bullshit. You were dishonorably discharged."

He shifted his weight and fell back on his old excuse. "It was a misunderstanding. And I *did* have problems from all the fighting."

"You worked supply unit."

He sneered at me. "What do you know about it? You were just a kid, you weren't there."

He was getting loud. I certainly didn't want the girls to hear him and have another episode like the day before when the package was delivered. I walked over, grabbed his arm and hustled him outside, closing the door firmly behind me.

"I'm not giving you money, so if that's why you came you made the trip for nothing. I'm not kidding, you need to get going, Dad. I'm busy and you're in the way."

"Fine!" he retorted in a tight voice. "Be that way. My own son."

"A fact you only remember when it's convenient. Go the fuck away."

His eyes narrowed at me and I saw him ball his hands into hard fists. Maybe that worked when I was a kid, but I was stronger than him now and wasn't putting up with any of his old bullshit. He saw it in my eyes and relaxed again.

"Okay, I'm going."

I didn't trust him, so I stood outside and watched until he got back in his car and drove away.

Fuck, I wanted him out of my life. He'd look good six feet under. If he didn't stay away that was a fate I'd make sure he'd meet. I should've done it long ago.

I trudged back into the house and this time made sure the door was firmly locked.

33

Addison

It was the worst yet. He was so violent I thought he was going to break me. I had to clamp my teeth together to keep from screaming. I could tell he was getting off on hurting me, and when he came his whole body shook, and he grunted with an animal growl.

He dropped his head onto my shoulder and I looked up at the bedroom ceiling almost in shock from the assault, though I should've have become used to his cruel savagery by then. He raised his head again and moved it so close to mine I thought he was going to kiss me, which made my skin crawl. The thought of his lips on mine made me feel physically sick.

"Tell me you liked it," he whispered.

I opened my mouth as if to speak — and bit his lip as hard as I could. I felt blood trickle down my chin. He howled with rage and pain.

It was a terrible mistake. He hit my face with a closed fist so hard I almost passed out. I was forced to release my hold on his lip. He reared up and hit me again. Then again. My vision began to blur.

He said, "You just won't learn."

It was the last thing I heard before I passed out.

When I finally came to I was disoriented, unsure of where I was. It took me a minute but I realized I was still in the bedroom. I was surprised I hadn't been banished to the dog cage again, but grateful for the fact. The very thought of it made me shudder.

I had no idea how long I'd been unconscious. I glanced at the shutters but it was still light out. It might have been late in the afternoon, but I wasn't sure.

The left side of my face hurt badly. I raised my hand and explored it gently. It was puffy, and even though I barely touched it there was a severe, sharp pain wherever my fingers brushed it. He'd hit me so hard I feared some of the bone might have splintered or broken, but as I felt my way across the planes of my face I didn't think so. There would be bad bruises, I was sure, as well as a black eye. My left eye was swollen and I had a hard time seeing past the outraged flesh. I wished I had a mirror so I could see the damage. Then I decided maybe it was just as well I didn't. I probably didn't want to know.

I curled up into a ball and fought the tears that came despite my attempt at self-control. I felt so defeated. I could tell I was coming close to real despair, but I knew if I allowed myself to give into it I would never leave this house of horrors. Up to now I'd remained determined not to give up. I *will* escape him, I told myself firmly. But part of my mind refused to believe it was possible anymore. That part whispered I was nothing but a tiny, vulnerable kitten being tormented by a vicious boy, and had as much a chance of getting away as it did.

The sound of the door opening made me cringe involuntarily.

He thrust Cheryl into the room and shut and locked the door behind her.

Her eyes widened at the sight of me.

"Holy god!" she whispered. She just stood there a moment, as if unsure what to do.

"I look that good, huh?" I croaked.

"Jesus. I'm so sorry, Addison."

"Not as sorry as I am."

Finally she broke her paralysis and came and sat on the end of the bed. "How bad does it hurt?" she asked.

"You can probably guess," I answered. "He's beaten you before."

She said nothing. I glanced over at her and saw the haunted look in her eyes and quickly looked away again. It reminded me too much of my own melancholy state of mind.

Finally I said, "I wonder if this is ever going to end." I laughed bitterly, and didn't like the hint of hysteria I heard in it. "Loss after loss. I once thought everything I cared about was gone. And then this. I wouldn't have believed it was possible to lose anything more, but I have. My freedom, my dignity, my confidence… I'm not sure I'll ever feel safe again."

She seemed to pull herself together, maybe for me. "We'll get out of this. You'll get your life back, Addison."

I shook my head. "I'll never get it back. Not really."

She put a hand on my knee. "You'll carry scars, Addison, but wounds heal."

I did look at her then. I smiled wryly and quickly stopped as my lower lip began to bleed. I dabbed at it with my finger.. "You said that well. Almost as good as *my* shrink might have." I paused and thought of those far away sessions where I sat and poured my heart out to someone who was a stranger. "Wounds don't heal, Cheryl. There's just less of you that wakes up every morning."

She studied me for a moment then asked, “Why were you seeing someone?”

I wanted to bury my head in the pillow but it hurt too much. I wanted to run from the room and hide myself, but of course that was impossible. Anything but dredge up that long ago afternoon. But the memory I’d tried to escape for so long came boiling up in my mind’s eye, and the pain was still as fresh and raw as it was then.

“Three years ago,” I said in quivering voice, “We had a terrible thunderstorm. It was awful. It was coming down in sheets, taking trees down and stuff like that. My son… Justin… he was five years old. He was at a play date at a friend’s house. I had the flu, and I was sick as a dog, so Matt — my husband — he went to pick Justin up for me. On the way home….”

I stopped and gulped in air because my chest tightened so badly it felt like I couldn’t breathe. Cheryl said nothing, just waited patiently for me to continue. Finally I was able to bring myself back under control. I went on, my voice sounding odd, like it belonged to a stranger.

“On the way home an oncoming truck hydroplaned on the drenched pavement and lost control… Matt….”

Tears began washing down my face. I felt Cheryl take my hand.

“I didn’t know they made caskets that small,” I finished in a bare whisper.

Cheryl folded me into her arms and rocked me gently like a baby. I let the tears flow and broke out into loud hiccupping sobs. After what felt like an eternity the hot wave of emotion finally ebbed and I remained in her arms, drained.

“I’m so sorry, honey,” she crooned over and over.

I stayed there a moment then pulled slowly away. She reached over and lifted a hank of hair that had fallen over the unhurt side of my face.

“That was a horrible tragedy, to be sure. It’s not easy to get over something like that.”

"I'll never get over it. I feel so guilty. If I had gone instead of sending Matt—"

"You'd be the one buried in the ground instead. It wasn't your fault, Addison. Sometimes bad things happen. Don't let the memory ruin your life. And don't let *this* ruin it either."

"I just can't seem to get a handle on it," I replied shakily. "This situation — *him* — just proves to me I never will be able to get things together again. I couldn't stop that accident from happening. Ever since then I've only let things into my life that I can control. But I was kidding myself. No matter how hard I try, I'll never be able to control a damned thing in my life. This situation is proof of that."

After a moment she said, "Survive. That's how you do it, Addison. Do it for them, for their memory. For the bright moments of your life you had with them, and the ones that will come again. Matt and Justin deserve for you to continue on."

34

Cheryl

Survivor's guilt is just what it sounds like. Someone close to you dies or goes through a horrible crisis, and the survivor immediately thinks, 'Why them, why not me?' And they feel deep emotional pain that they're still here while the other person isn't. Soldiers experience this a lot. The guy next to you is shot and killed, and the soldier wonders at the unfairness of it all. They think they should've saved them somehow, so they feel responsible for their death.

It's not rational, but honestly, so many of our thoughts and reactions to the things life throws us aren't.

People who suffer from this often withdraw from society, even close friends and family.

Which is why, after hearing her story, I was surprised Addison was still fighting Daddy so hard. The loss of a spouse and a child would numb most people, making them easy for someone like him to tame. Being kidnapped so close on the heels of a tragedy like hers would make a lot of people give up. Abused teens I'd had sessions with decided early on that Life was against them, and they didn't get it this time around, so why bother? What was the point in fighting for anything?

Usually you have two kinds of reactions to a situation like ours; some have the inherent fight-or-flight instinct, and others freeze like a fawn, feeling lack of control, or because of a past trauma, like those teens. Which is why I would've thought Addison belonged in the second category.

At the moment I watched her, curled up on the bed, her face a mess after being hit by Daddy, looking exhausted by grief and constant fear. And no wonder. It easy to break under the weight of the dread and hopelessness.

However, she still defied and fought Daddy fiercely.

I knew she thought I was either a complete coward, or I had Stockholm Syndrome. I knew I didn't, but it was hard to convince her otherwise. I didn't call out when that delivery guy knocked at the door, but sometimes you can't move or call out, like those dreams where you're paralyzed. I said that to her, but knew she didn't completely buy it.

But just because I was a psychologist didn't mean I was infallible. I had made plenty of bad judgement calls in my life. I was living the repercussions of one now.

35

Detective Kennedy

Once again I looked at the fingerprint report on Addison Clifton's car, which currently sat in the department's compound yard. There were quite a few prints that belonged to her, and some that turned out to be Barbara Meade's. Made sense since they were close friends. There was some unidentified male prints, which seemed promising.

We tracked the guy down but it was a bust, they ended up belonging to her mechanic, and he'd worked for her for years apparently. He also had a pretty solid alibi for the time frame she went missing, he was on vacation in Florida with his wife. I tossed it aside, frustrated. No help there.

Lemuche and I circled back to the five HookedUp suspects we'd already questioned and put them through it all again. It was pretty normal procedure; we just wanted to see if their stories changed at all. They didn't.

Meanwhile, I went back to the motel clerk to see if he remembered anything new. I probed him over every little detail, but he couldn't recall anything past what he'd already told us. I reviewed the motel's camera footage, but the only place it captured footage was the check-in office, and Addison was the only person on it that night other than two couples. The first was a man and woman in their mid-thirties, and the other couple were senior citizens.

I got on the National Missing and Unidentified Persons System to see if there was anything new. We use it to cross reference missing persons with unidentified remains. Not the outcome we hoped for, but the reality was a possibility. There was nothing, which I guess was somewhat reassuring. Unless of course she had been killed and her body hadn't been found.

It seemed like we were hitting a brick wall wherever we turned.

It was past seven when Lemuche walked in and plopped into his chair. He ran his fingers through his hair, a nervous habit he often did whenever he got frustrated.

"I think we need to back burn this one," he said.

I looked up, surprised. "A missing person takes precedence. You know that."

"But we're not getting anywhere. And frankly I don't see any other leads, do you? We've tracked her movements since she had brunch with Meade all the way to the night she met up with our mystery man. Since then everything else has checked out. Until we hear from IT on who he is I don't see much else to do. Last I checked they weren't having much success."

I actually knew that, I'd talked to them that morning myself. I had to admit it was frustrating.

"Anyway, we've got a backlog here," he continued, "And I think we should move onto something else until we ID the guy."

I knew he was probably right, but I was loathe to surrender the search right then. Something told me we'd find her sooner than later if we kept at it.

Just then Wycowski put his head in the door.

"Hey, Kennedy!" he called.

"Yeah?"

"I got a guy out front you might want to talk to."

"Yeah? Why?"

"Something about a screaming woman."

I looked over at Lemuche. He shrugged. "Okay. Send him back," I told Wycowski.

The man who approached us was a thin black male. He looked to be in his mid-forties. He seemed nervous about being in the bull pen. I waved him over. He stopped by our desks and looked all around, a slight tic pulling at one side of his mouth.

"I'm Detective Kennedy, and this is my partner, Detective Lemuche. How can we help you?" I asked pleasantly, trying to put him at ease.

He cleared his throat and said, "My name's Scott Bushey. I'm a delivery driver for UPS."

"Would you like to sit down?" I asked, waving him to an adjacent chair.

He did, sitting on the edge, his back ruler straight, poised as if to make a quick getaway. He cleared his throat again. "Well, yesterday I made a delivery and I heard something that sounded… well, suspicious. It's been weighing on my mind, so I thought I'd better tell someone."

"Yes? Go on," I urged.

"I had to get a signature for a package, see. I knocked and the guy who lived there told me to leave it, but when I said I needed his signature he acted pissed or something. I had to wait a few minutes, then he finally came to the door. He was acting all weird, you know. Antsy like. Then I heard a woman screaming inside. He got all flustered then and quickly signed, told me it was just the TV. He shut the door real fast after that."

"Was it just a scream, or did the woman call out for help?" I asked.

"She was screaming something about being kidnapped. That kinda creeped me out, you know?"

"*Could* it have been the TV?" asked Lemuche.

"Well… maybe," he replied thoughtfully then looked at both of us, his face serious. "But it sure didn't sound that way to me. Sounded awfully real and close by."

"You said this happened yesterday," said Lemuche gruffly. "Why did you wait till now to tell somebody?"

Mr. Bushey cringed slightly. Lemuche often had that effect. "I didn't know what to do. A woman yelling she's been kidnapped, well that seems kinda unbelievable, you know? I mean, things like that don't happen. I just passed it off as being tired after a long day, and maybe it really was just some movie or TV program, or maybe he and his lady were having a fight and she was trying to get him in trouble. I didn't know, but I didn't want to jump the gun and get myself in trouble with my job. But like I said, I've kept on thinking about it, and the more I have the more it's troubled me."

He stopped and looked at me like he was hoping I'd pat him on the back or something. I nodded.

"You were right to come to us, Mr. Bushey. Do you remember the address where this occurred?"

He nodded. "We keep logs on our DIAD, that's a digital thing we use to track what we're doing. I also keep a manual logbook. I checked it and wrote it down for you."

He dug into one of his front pockets and passed a folded piece of paper to me. I unfolded it. 1906 Wright Rd., Trouville. I passed it over to Lemuche and turned my attention back to the driver.

"Thank you, sir. We're going to need your contact information in case we have to get back in touch with you. Also, if this turns into a criminal case then you might be called to testify in court."

He nodded again, gave me all of his information, then stood up. I held out my hand and he shook it. Then he left very quickly, looking like he wanted to run.

When I looked back at Lemuche he was staring at the address intently.

"Do you know where that is?" I asked him.

He jumped a little, like I startled him. "Hm? Oh, sorry. No, I don't, but I think I know the area." He tossed the paper aside. "Sounds farfetched to me. If I had kidnapped a woman I'd keep her somewhere where no one could hear her. Like a basement or a cabin in the middle of the woods, not just inside where a delivery guy could hear her."

I stood up and put on my coat jacket. "Maybe. But I think we need to check it out anyway."

His eyes widened in surprise. "Us? This isn't detective work, Kennedy. Why don't we just send a patrol car?"

I smiled at him. "You wanted a break in the Clifton case? This might be it."

"What're the chances?"

I frowned at him. "We won't know until we check it out, will we? Come on."

He scowled, but rose and put on his own jacket. "I still think we should just send a patrol."

"Stop bitching. I'll drive."

"No, I'll drive. But I gotta hit the head first. Meet you at the car."

When I stepped out of the bullpen I noticed the front desk was empty. Where was Wycowski? I glanced out of the window and saw him outside on his cell phone, standing with his back to me and puffing on a cigarette.

I shrugged. He was a smoker and stepped out every now and then. He wasn't supposed to, but who was I to judge. Besides the front room was empty at the moment.

A couple minutes later Lemuche returned.

“Let’s go,” he said.

36

Addison

After the beating he'd given me I expected more rough treatment, so I was surprised when he came into the room and invited Cheryl and me to dinner with him again. I was beginning to think he wasn't just psychotic but bipolar as well. His mood swings were all over the place. I guessed there was really no difference between the two in his case.

We sat in our usual chairs, our ankles cuffed once again to a table leg.

The table was set more elegantly than before. Well, if plastic plates and bowls could be called elegant. But he had a small plastic vase of flowers and two candles on the table. They weren't real, of course, with real flames. They were those plastic things with LEDs to simulate the flicker effect. Probably because he knew I'd pick up a real lit candle and try to stab him in the eye with it.

There were wine glasses at each place setting as well, plastic naturally.

There was a soft pop as he uncorked a bottle of wine and filled all of our glasses. The thought briefly crossed my mind that he might be trying to get us drunk, then I laughed inwardly. As if he'd have to. He forced himself on us whenever he wanted.

I stared at the plastic spoons at his and Cheryl's settings — naturally I had not been given silverware, even plastic — and wondered if it would break if I tried to stab him with one. Obviously. Anyway, it would just get me another beating and one was enough for the day. The left side of my face was throbbing painfully from being so swollen. I could barely see out of my left eye.

He stood at his chair and raised his glass. "This is an excellent Pinot Noir. Salute!" He took a drink then looked from one to the other of us expecting Cheryl and me to follow suit.

She immediately took a large gulp of hers. "It's good," she said to him.

He looked pointedly at me. I raised the glass and took a small sip, watching him carefully over the rim of the glass. I sat it back down and said nothing.

He gave me a blank look that gave no hint of what he was thinking, then he abruptly turned and went into the kitchen. He pulled a heavy oven mitt onto one hand, lifted a heavy ceramic cooking pot and a ladle, and returned to the table with them. He ladled a rich aromatic beef stew into Cheryl's bowl then headed for me.

I cringed back, half expecting him to ladle the steaming hot stuff onto my lap or over my head, the tea incident still fresh in my mind. He noticed my reaction and a small smile appeared on his lips. Bastard.

He held the ladle out for just a moment, creating suspense, then dropped the contents into my plastic bowl. He then served himself, returned the pot to the kitchen and came back to sit with us.

I stared at the food in front of me. It smelled wonderful, but the thought foremost in my mind was picking it up and flinging the contents into his face. I was actually reaching for it when the ache in my face reminded me of the consequences of such an action. I dropped my hand back into my lap and cursed myself for my lack of courage.

He picked up his spoon and nodded to each of us. "Boeuf Bourguignon, ladies. Bon appetite."

He and Cheryl began eating. I stared at it. It was steaming, obviously too hot to touch with my fingers, which was all I had. I wondered if he had placed it there to torture me. I was hungry but unable to join them.

"It's my own recipe," he said. He looked at Cheryl. "What do you think?"

"It's delicious," she answered.

He gave me a questioning look. He knew why I wasn't eating, and there was a taunt in his eyes.

"Why're you doing all this?" was all I said in response to his look.

He shrugged and took another bite. After he'd swallowed he said, "Every good cook wants people to share and like his food."

"I can't *share* your food when it's this hot, and you know it." I slammed my fist on the table, causing the stew in my bowl to slop over the rim. "I'm not some doll at a child's tea party, dammit, so stop playing stupid games!"

He just gave me another one of those blank stares. It was such a dead look it made me tremble inside.

Once again I felt the fight and resistance in me drain away, leaving me feeling hollow and defeated. "Just get it over with," I said in a dull voice.

He raised his eyebrows in surprise. "Get what over with?"

"Whatever horrible thing you're planning to do."

Suddenly he smiled, mentally waving my comment away and returned to his meal. "Dinner conversation should be light, don't you think?" he asked casually.

I said nothing in return, just stared vacantly at my bowl.

"All right," he said with a sigh and pushed himself away from the table. "I'd hate for you to miss out on such an excellent meal."

He opened a drawer and returned with a small plastic spoon which he held out to me. I reached for it but he pulled it back, just out of my reach, raising his eyebrows at me. What did he want me to say? Thank you?

His cell phone suddenly rang. He tossed the spoon at me, pulled his cell from his pocket and looked at the caller ID. "Hey," he greeted the caller, obviously someone he knew. "Hold on a sec." He looked down at me. "I suggest you eat and drink your wine. I went to a lot of trouble to make it. Unless you're in the mood for more tea."

He left the kitchen, disappearing into the living room. I could hear him speaking in a low voice but couldn't make out any words.

The minute he was out of sight Cheryl leaned over her bowl and hissed, "Addison, don't. Why do you keep trying to piss him off?"

Because I hated him. "Because I hate him," I replied.

"Just stop it already. You piss him off too much and he might hurt me too. And Addison… I'm tired of being hurt."

"I'm not trying to get you hurt," I said in a tired voice.

"Then stop mouthing off," she commanded. "You need to try and engage him, get him on our side."

"Hah!" I replied sarcastically. "If he were on our side, Cheryl, we wouldn't be here."

She sat back and glanced toward the living room to make sure he was still out of hearing then looked at me seriously. "Has it ever occurred to you that if we try to make him our friend and not our adversary, he might see us as people and not objects to fuck. It might make him let his guard down a little so we can make a strategic move to get out of here. So maybe instead of fighting him all the time we should try and reach his heart."

I returned her look incredulously. Finally, I said, "He'd have to have one."

Once again I began to doubt where her mind was. She was my only ally, but sometimes it felt like she was almost protecting him. Again my thoughts drifted to the Stockholm Syndrome. Had he beaten her down so thoroughly? She couldn't really believe we could appeal to his humanity. I doubted he had any. At least not where we were concerned.

"Just try," she pleaded in a whisper.

I slowly shook my head. "I don't think I can. I really don't."

"Okay, look… you were right before. I blew it when the package was delivered, but I'm gonna try harder. But if you want out of here you have to help me."

"How?" So far all her suggestions were out of the question for me.

"Start trusting me, for one. Remember, I've been here longer. Maybe I've had more time to think things out about our situation."

Suddenly he reappeared in the kitchen. He looked angry.

"Fun time's over," he said.

37

Detective Kennedy

It was close to dark when we pulled into the driveway of 1906 Wright Street, and we could hear loud music playing even through our closed windows. It was a medium-sized ranch house and it seemed rather isolated; there were no neighbors for several miles in any direction. Then I caught sight of a man in the garage. The light was on, the hood of his car was up and he appeared to be working on it.

As we got out and neared him I could see it was an old car, one of those boxy Volvo sedans from the 1980's or 90's. He looked up at our approach, wiping off his hands with an old rag. He raised his eyebrows in a question.

"Hello," he said tentatively. "Can I help you?"

He appeared to be in his mid to late thirties and had a strong build. His eyes were travelling from me to Lemuche at the moment, unsure.

"Sir," I called, having to raise my voice over the music, "Could you turn down the music and step outside for a moment."

"I'm sorry, but who are you?" he called.

Lemuche and I stepped forward, both pulling out our badges and holding them out to him for inspection. He looked at them, perplexed, then back at the two of us.

"Is something wrong?"

"Can you please turn down the music?" I asked again.

He nodded, stepped around the car, hit mute on his phone and returned to us.

"I'm Detective Kennedy and this is Detective Lemuche," I said.

Lemuche stared at the man mutely. It unsettled many people, which is why I suspect he often did it. This man didn't appear to be affected that way though. He just smiled politely and waited for one of us to explain our visit.

"Do you live here?" I asked.

He nodded. "Yes."

"What is your name, sir?"

"Max Jondo," he replied, then asked again, "Is something wrong, detectives?"

"Do you live alone?" I asked.

"Yeah, why?"

"Have you had any female visitors lately?"

He shook his head. "No."

"We got a tip there's been a disturbance involving a woman at this address."

He opened his eyes in surprise. "Here? That's… you must be mistaken. I haven't had anyone here in ages, I promise. Just me."

"Are there any sheds or outbuildings here, sir?"

He seemed confused. "No. Look around, you can see."

"So it's just the house?" He nodded. "Would you mind if I went inside and looked around, Mr. Jondo?"

He looked from me to Lemuche, who still remained expressionless. Finally he said, "Well... what're you looking for?"

"You don't have to give me permission, of course, but in that case I will come back with a warrant," I replied.

"I don't understand. I haven't done anything," he said, narrowing his eyes.

"Then you shouldn't mind my going inside and looking around," I said.

He sighed and tossed his rag onto a nearby work table, then started for the door. "This way."

I gave Lemuche a look and nodded toward Jondo. He got my message.

"Mr. Jondo," he said. "Please wait out here with me."

Jondo stopped abruptly and looked back at him a long moment, then finally said, "Okay." To me he said, "Right through there." He motioned to a door in the garage.

"Thank you," I replied and stepped inside.

Just before I closed the door I heard him ask Lemuche nervously, "What is he hoping to find?"

The door led to a modest kitchen with an eat-in area filled with a table and three chairs. The kitchen looked innocuous enough. I could see the remains of his dinner sitting on the counter alongside a half full bottle of wine. A pot was sitting on the unlit stove. I inspected it and saw the remains of a stew of some sort. Innocent enough.

I took out my phone and snapped a quick picture of the kitchen and eating area, then ventured into the interior of the house. Beyond the kitchen was a long rectangular living room. There was a desk with a laptop and a lamp, a sofa and several chairs, but that was really it. Dark hard wood floors lay underneath. I continued down a hallway.

There was a full bathroom, but it seemed completely empty. The medicine cabinet was missing its mirror and was also empty.

Strange, I thought as I opened the cabinet beneath the sink, but it was also empty.

What alerted my senses was the fact the small window was completely sealed by strong metal shutters. I pulled on them but they were firmly bolted into the wall.

I was looking for any hint that Addison might have been kept there.

The next two bedrooms were very sparse. In each there was nothing but a small double bed. That was it, no lamps or anything personal at all. There were also the same shutters I'd seen in the bathroom. I opened the closets, but they were empty as well, and I shined my light under the beds but there was nothing other than a few dust bunnies.

The last bedroom was the largest and it was obviously Jondo's. It had a queen size bed, a dresser and all the things you'd expect to find in a bedroom. I went through the drawers and closet but there appeared to be nothing out of the ordinary.

The only thing left to explore was the basement.

I found the door in the kitchen and went down. The stairs were narrow and steep and I emerged into a dank and very dark room. I found the switch and a weak overhead light sent shadows running into the corners.

Besides a water tank and heater the large space was fairly empty. An old mattress was leaning up against one of the cinder block walls. I went over and inspected it but it appeared to be what it looked like. I rubbed my chin, a little perplexed. I saw a hole in the wall nearby, and it looked like it had recently held a heavy bolt or the like. I took multiple pictures and was about to leave again when I saw something in the shadows.

Upon inspection it was a large dog cage. I shone my light inside and saw an old leash lying inside. I gingerly picked it up but immediately saw that it couldn't have constrained anyone — it was frayed and almost worn in half in the middle. I tossed it back down.

I'd seen all I needed.

As I mounted the steps and crossed the kitchen something nagged at my mind. I felt I missed something but wasn't sure what it was.

Suddenly, I stopped and turned back to the basement.

I returned to the dog cage and shined my light on it again. There it was. It was easy to miss, and you had to catch it just right in the light to see it at all. I removed a small evidence bag from my jacket pocket and quickly bagged it up.

Outside I found Jondo and Lemuche still standing where I'd left them. Jondo was looking more nervous than before. Lemuche raised his eyebrows in a question. I shook my head slightly.

"Why do you have metal shutters on some of the windows?" I asked Jondo.

"I got broken into several times so I finally put them up as a safety."

"Only on three windows?"

He shrugged. "Haven't gotten around to the others, but not sure I will now. Things have quietened down after I put the first ones up," he said.

"I see," I said noncommittedly.

"What were you hoping to find?" he probed again.

"I'm not at liberty to disclose that, sir," I replied, dodging the question.

He stuck his hands in his pockets and looked between me and Lemuche. "So, is that it? I'm not in trouble or anything, am I?"

"Not at this time," was all I replied. "Sorry for the inconvenience. Good night, sir."

I motioned to Lemuche and we walked away, got in the car and backed out of the driveway.

"Find any evidence of our missing woman?" he asked.

"Not exactly," I replied slowly.

"What do you mean?" he asked, glancing over at me, suddenly alert.

I told him about my find in the basement.

He rolled his eyes. “A hair in a dog cage?” he scoffed. “Not exactly evidence, Kennedy.”

I just smiled. “We’ll see.”

He waved me away with a smile, then became serious again. “We may find her, but not back there. That was a total bust.” He took his eyes off the road and glanced at me. “Told you so.”

“Maybe. But the real question is, will we find her in time? It’s slipping away and I’m worried we might be too late.”

38

Daddy

I watched the detectives drive away. Although I was fairly sure I was in the clear I was seething inside.

That bitch!

I waited ten minutes to be sure the two men wouldn't return, then pulled the garage door down. I walked around the car and unlocked the trunk.

Addison was inside. A sufficient Ketamine injection knocks a person out pretty damn quick, especially when injected with a syringe. It's the second time I've used it on her, the first time being at our second motel hookup, only that time I spiked her drink with it. Ketamine is a guy's best friend.

Still, I leave nothing to chance, so I'd also tied and gagged her to be on the safe side. Apparently that was unnecessary, because she was still out cold. I opened the door to the kitchen and the door to the basement, then I returned and lifted Addison out. She often refused food and had lost some weight, so it wasn't a difficult task. However, she was getting too skinny, and I hated that on women. I was going to have to make her eat. I carried her to the basement.

Then I retrieved Cheryl, who had been stashed behind a dummy wall in my closet, and took her down as well.

I stood looking down at the two women lying together on the mattress. Addison's could've gotten me into serious fucking trouble this time, and it was only my fast thinking that saved my ass. That and the tip off I got during dinner. That was another thing that pissed me off, an excellent meal I'd worked hard on had been ruined because of her.

Looking at Addison's still face, I was torn.

I liked her, but it was time to get rid of her. She was more trouble than she was worth. Unfortunately, I wasn't able to do that just yet. It would come, and probably sooner than later if I had my way, but the time wasn't right. However, I was starting to look forward to it happening. Then she'd realize who she was dealing with, and the mistake she'd made in underestimating me.

My phone rang. I pulled it from my back pocket and glanced quickly down at the women. Neither stirred. Nevertheless, I didn't answer until I was back in the kitchen.

"Thanks for the heads up," I said.

"You need to clean your shit up, Max. If anyone finds out I tipped you off I'm in deep fucking trouble. So don't make me have to do it again."

He hung up on me.

I looked at my phone and shrugged. It didn't mean anything. I knew he'd always have my back.

I walked over to the stove and looked down at the cold congealed remains of my Boef Bourguignon. I felt myself get angry all over again. I picked it up and threw the whole thing, pot and all, into the garbage.

Fucking waste.

39

Barb

Detective Kennedy, how are you?" I inquired sweetly. "How's your vacation going? Getting a nice tan?"

"Um… excuse me?" he replied on the other end of the phone, confused.

"Well, you certainly haven't been *working*, that's clear. Where is Addison? Why haven't you fucking found her yet?"

Peter peeked out of his office and scowled at me. "Can you watch the language, Barb?"

I shot him the finger.

He sighed loudly. "At least keep your voice down. I got a meeting going on in here." He disappeared again quickly before I could say anything, firmly shutting his door behind him.

"Ms. Meade, I've already told you —" Kennedy began.

"I know what you've told me. It's a stale bit already."

"Ms. Meade —"

"What the hell have you and that beefcake partner of yours been doing? It's been a week now, dammit."

"I will tell you if you'll allow me to talk," he said, his voice strained.

I took a deep breath and counted to ten. "Fine," I said, trying to cool my jets a little. "Tell me."

"We got a tip from a delivery person about a woman screaming from inside a house he delivered a package to."

I sat up, suddenly alert. "And?"

"I'm sorry, it didn't pan out. However —"

"Whaddya mean, didn't pan out? Did you go inside?" I demanded. I could hear my voice getting loud again. I shrugged. Who cared.

"Yes, I did," he replied. I swear I could hear him counting under his breath.

I have that effect on people sometimes. I know how I can come across, but this was Addison's welfare, and it could very well be her life at stake. So who gave two fucks what Kennedy thought of me?

"Did you check everywhere?" I wanted to know. "I mean, someone who's going to go to the trouble to abduct a woman is going to be crafty. Chain her in the basement, attic or in a remote shed hidden in the woods. Maybe even have a hidey-hole in their house. You checked *everywhere*? Knocked on the walls to see if there was a hidden room? That sort of thing?"

He actually chuckled. "You've been reading too many mysteries, Ms. Meade. Those sorts of things don't exist."

"If I were going to kidnap someone that's what I would do. Obviously *you* didn't discover anything." Then I had a depressing thought. "Please tell me it wasn't just some stupid domestic fight the delivery dude overheard?"

"No, it wasn't. The gentleman who resides there said he was single and hadn't received any female guests."

“Then what about all the screaming?”

“He maintained it was his television,” he replied.

I snorted in derision. “Oh, give me a break! His TV? Even a two year old can the difference between a TV and a real person. Did this delivery guy seem like a moron to you?”

“No, ma’am.”

“So there you are,” I said smugly. “That means he really heard a woman screaming. It could’ve been Addison.” Then an idea struck me. “What if it really was her and he just moved her somewhere else before you got there? Ever think of that?” Hell, he was the detective but *I* was coming up with the better theories. “Maybe you should’ve checked his car for clues. Like torn pieces of clothing, strands of her hair or …blood spots.”

He was silent a moment, then said slowly, “Ms. Meade, I know you’re worried, and I know it’s difficult to have to remain in the dark, but I promise we’re working diligently on Addison’s case. I’m already telling you a lot more than I should, but frankly I know you’ll just keep calling so I decided to give you our latest progress first. I’ve told you everything going on at present, so I’d appreciate it if you’d back off a little and let us do our job.”

“So I’m just supposed to sit on my hands over here and do nothing?” I asked sourly.

“I’ll let you know the minute we get a break in the case,” he said in a too patient a voice, like I was an unhinged person he was trying to calm down.

He hadn’t seen me unhinged yet. Then I got an idea.

“Where was this house?” I asked, trying my best to sound innocently curious.

He chuckled again. “Nice try. I have to be going, Ms. Meade. Thanks for calling.”

The bastard hung up.

I sat at my desk, glowering at the silent phone and conjuring up all the gruesome ways I'd like to torture him and that Lemuche prick.

Then unexpectantly I felt my eyes begin to sting as tears formed.

Addison, where are you, I begged silently? I wasn't much of a prayer, but at that moment I prayed with all my heart that she was okay, that she wasn't being hurt, that she was alive.

Please, God, let her be alive.

40

Addison

When I came to I heard soft moaning nearby. I forced my eyes open. Everything was blurry and it took a minute for my vision to clear. The moaning persisted. The lines of cobweb draped pipes overhead made me realize I was once again in the basement. I felt beneath me, I was lying on the dank mattress, and I was being held by the chain again.

I felt something stir nearby and looked over. It was Cheryl.

She was blinking up at the ceiling.

I struggled to sit up and was immediately overcome by dizziness. I let myself fall back down again.

"Are you okay?" I asked. My throat felt like someone had used a cheese grater on it.

"My throat hurts," she replied. "My head, too."

"I know, same here." I swallowed hard, wishing I had some water. "What happened?" I asked.

"I don't know for sure," she replied, and was immediately overtaken by a fit of coughing. "He took a syringe out of his pocket, came up behind you and injected you with something. It was scary how fast it knocked you out. Then he turned on me and that's all I remember. But my muscles are all stiff and sore."

"Yeah, but… why?" I asked. "He's never done anything like that before. I'm horrified to think what he did to us when we were unconscious."

She shook her head. "I don't know. It must've had something to do with that phone call he got."

I remembered that now, and also how angry he seemed when he returned to the kitchen. My mind began to fly in circles. Maybe someone at the motel finally remembered him and called the cops.

The bastard.

He must've drugged us to keep from calling out. I wanted to scream in frustration, but my throat was so raw I could barely croak. To think we'd been that close to rescue made me want to cry.

But… how would he know that? The police wouldn't call him and say they were on the way. I sighed deeply. Shit, I was wrong, and it was simply wishful thinking on my part. I'd already been missing for some time, and even that idiot clerk at the motel wouldn't wait this long to identify the man I met there.

Then it struck me. The clerk *couldn't* identify him. I checked in alone, something I did for security. I didn't want anyone to know I was meeting someone else, and I didn't want the men I met to know my real name. After checking in I messaged the room number to him, so he never would've gone to the front office at all. Another hope dashed. And once again it was all my own fault.

My god, I'd made so many bad decisions.

So… why would he have to silence us if the police never came? Was it someone else? Someone he didn't want to know that we were here?

I heard heavy footsteps overhead, followed by the basement door creaking open.

I was about to find out.

"You want me to do what?"

I was standing at one end of the basement, holding a pair of handcuffs in my hands.

Across the room he crouched next to Cheryl, who was still sitting on the mattress, but now had her leg fixed to the chain in the wall. She looked nervously between him and me.

"Turn around and cuff yourself to that pipe above your head," he replied in an odd nonchalant voice.

I looked at the pipe he referred to then back at him, shaking my head. "No."

He nodded as if he had expected that answer. He dug into one of his pockets and pulled out a pocketknife. He opened it and looked up at me again, smiling. He casually put an arm around Cheryl's shoulder.

"Here's the thing, Addison. Someone has got to pay for you shouting to that delivery guy and getting the cops sent here."

I was right! The cops did come while we were unconscious! That's why he had to silence us.

"He continued. "Either you…."

He tested the knife on his thumb and a tiny drop of blood appeared. He held it at Cheryl's throat and looked steadily at me.

"… Or her," he finished.

My heart felt like it stopped, and my throat closed up in fear.

"You wouldn't," I whispered.

"Do you really want to find out?"

"Addis—" began Cheryl, but she was stopped as he clutched her jaw and yanked her head toward him. The knife dug into her throat and a tiny bead of blood appeared. Cheryl whimpered.

"Question wasn't for you," he said to her. He turned back to me. "What you've got coming isn't gonna be fun …but it's not like her getting her throat slit. Now turn around and cuff yourself to that pipe."

My chest hurt and I was having a hard time breathing. I was vacillating between fear and fury. I glared at him a moment then turned around and reached up.

He stopped me by saying, "Drop that robe first. It'll be hard to put back on if I have to cut it off of you."

I wanted to run over and scratch his eyes out, to kick him in the face, but I took a deep breath and controlled myself. I also controlled my tongue, biting back an ugly retort. I couldn't let him kill Cheryl, and from the look in his eyes I could tell he'd do it. She was shaking with fear, looking at me with huge eyes.

I untied the belt and slowly let the robe slip from my shoulders and slide down to the floor. I shivered, naked and chilled by the cool, dank air. Then I reached up and fixed one end of the cuffs to the pipe. I hesitated, then I closed the other end around my wrist. I closed my eyes, trying to slow my heart, which was racing out of control.

I heard him rise and slowly walk toward me. My arm was stretched to the limit and was beginning to ache. He was making noise and I finally realized he was unbuckling his belt. Oh, shit.

"Very simple rules in this house," he said. "But you have to go out of your way to break them, don't you?"

He let a finger run softly down my back, stopping just above the spot where he had scalded me with the tea. I jerked, surprised by the touch.

"You know what the most important rule is, don't you?" he asked quietly.

I began to breathe heavily and suddenly I was filled with a rage I'd never experienced before. It was like something exploded inside me.

"Fuck you!"

I kicked back at him with all the strength I had. I made contact with one of his shins, and felt him being pushed backward by the force of my assault.

He cried out in pain and anger, but the bastard recovered quickly.

The belt whistled through the air as it came whipping down upon on my back.

41

Addison

When he uncuffed my wrist I fell to the floor in a wobbly heap. I lay on the cold cement floor, sobbing uncontrollably. My back was on fire. The pain was like shattered glass had been embedded in every inch of my skin. I didn't know how much more of this torture I could take.

Out of the corner of my eye I could see Cheryl looking at me with horror and pity in her eyes.

Then I felt his hand on my shoulder and I stiffened.

"Get up," he said.

I slowly raised to all fours, then got painfully to my feet. He took my arm and guided me over to the dog cage, which was now stuffed back in a dark corner of the room.

"You'll be staying here tonight. Get in," he commanded.

I felt dizzy and was about to fall again, so I reached for the top of the cage to steady myself. I could barely hold myself up and swayed dangerously.

"Get in," he repeated gruffly.

I took a deep breath, got onto my knees again and crawled inside, being careful to not let the mesh of the cage scrape against my raw back. I maneuvered around until I was facing him again. He hooked the bike lock around the latch and was about to snap it closed when he stopped. He crouched down and regarded me through the wire mesh.

"You know… I might be persuaded to let you come back upstairs and sleep in that comfortable bed… if you just say the magic word," he said softly.

I fixed on his eyes, those weird gray eyes. They held mine, mesmerizing me, though everything about the man utterly repulsed me. Then I mentally shook myself, forcing my eyes away from his. I was going to kill him, and I would enjoy it with all the fierce primal joy of an ancient hunter. They did it for sustenance or ritual, I would do it for revenge.

"The first chance I get, I'm going to kill you," I said flatly.

He smiled a huge grin then snapped the lock closed. He rose and walked away.

"Come on, Cheryl," he said casually. "It's just you and me tonight, babe."

I heard the snap of her release, followed by their footsteps ascending the stairs. Before he closed the door he hit the switch, and I was blanketed by a darkness that felt menacing. I waited to make sure he wasn't going to return then let my head drop into my hands. My whole body shook from the force of those breath stealing tears.

Eventually the crying subsided and I gulped in the chilly air to steady myself. I wished I had my robe, it was cold and my back throbbed painfully. My thirst was also becoming torture again. But there was nothing I could do about any of this at that moment. I was trapped in a cage, both literally and figuratively.

Somewhere I heard a soft scratching sound and was suddenly alert. I listened intently, then I heard it again. A mouse? Or worse yet, a rat? I'd spent a night down here before but never heard anything like that. The sound came again, but this time it was closer. I shied back against the cage but yelped when the thick wire came into contact with my blistered skin.

Moonlight escaping a cloud filtered its way through the high, dusty window across the room. That's when I saw it. Illuminated by the sudden light, a small pair of eyes regarded me from several feet away.

I screamed hoarsely and shied back again, not caring about my back this time. It was definitely a rodent of some kind.

I began to tremble violently. If it chose to scuttle inside the cage I had no way to defend myself from it. Did rats carry rabies? I didn't know. But the thought of it crawling over me made me writhe inside.

It scampered quickly forward towards my cage and I screamed again and began violently beating against the door to scare it away. It seemed to work, for the eyes suddenly disappeared. I looked frantically all around, frightened that it would try to come in another way. I had horrible visions of it coming in from behind and starting to nibble at the tender flesh of my back. Terror overtook me and I pushed my fingers through the cage and shook it as hard as I could but it did no good.

The moon disappeared again and the room was once more plunged in darkness. I pulled my knees up tightly in my arms and strained my eyes looking around the inky dark room.

I couldn't see it anymore but I heard it moving around somewhere. Every time I heard the little claws scrape the floor I flinched a little.

It was going to be a very long night.

42

Addison

When I woke it was to the sound of rain beating on the tiny window. It was grey and gloomy in the basement. I remembered the rat and flinched, sitting up and looking all around, but I didn't see it anywhere. I had stayed awake most of the night, and my eyes felt swollen and itched terribly. My mouth was like sawdust, my thirst was killing me, and my tongue felt swollen in my dry mouth.

Suddenly the overhead light came on, and I heard the thud of heavy footsteps coming down the stairs. I gathered my knees up again into my arms, covering some of my nakedness, and waited.

He walked past the cage, gathered up an old small wooden crate, brought it over and sat down upon it. He opened a tiny overhead hinged piece of the cage and handed me a plastic bottle of water. I snatched at it, my hands trembling as I opened it and drank desperately. When I'd drunk two thirds of it I looked back at him and saw he was watching me expressionlessly.

I returned his gaze sullenly.

Finally he said, "You just refuse to toe the line, don't you?"

"You're a sick man," I croaked. "You know that, right?"

"No," he replied. "I'm not. I'm your Daddy."

"You're not my father," I spit at him.

He shook his head. "Didn't say that. A father and a daddy are two different things. Any jerk can be a father, but it takes a special kind of man to be a good daddy."

I studied him a moment. "Is that why you're like this?" I asked.

"Like what?"

"A twisted, misogynistic bastard. Was it your father that made you like this? What, didn't he give you enough hugs? My father ran out on me and my mother after I was born, but I don't go around torturing people. Face it, you're a psychopath."

He rested his arms on his knees and leaned forward. He looked right into my eyes.

"You want to know about my father?" he said. "He's an asshole. He's a drunk and a gambler. My mother, my half-brother and I went hungry for his gambling debts. When I was ten I had a paper route, but he stole my money when I was asleep, so I gave it up. And believe me, I paid for that in other ways. A family's gotta eat, right?

"We all suffered, each of us in our own way. My dad would come home drunk and beat all of us, especially my mother. The last time he beat her so hard she couldn't get out of bed for two days. She got in the bathtub several nights later and slit her wrists. My half-brother found her the next morning."

He paused again, looking down at the floor then looked back at me. "And you want to know what I thought when I looked at her pale naked body lying in that pool of bloody water? I thought, 'You selfish bitch. Selfish, selfish bitch.' I couldn't stand my father. But I really hated her."

He pulled the crate closer and leaned in, his face almost touching the cage door.

"Maybe you should be worrying about your half of the equation instead of worrying about how many hugs I got from my father."

He got up then and left, his footfalls slow and heavy on the stairs. He flipped the switch and I was once again swallowed by the grey murkiness of the basement.

Why did he tell me all of that? Was I supposed to feel sorry for him? No way. But it troubled me. I didn't think he would be telling personal details about his life unless my days here were numbered, and that meant only one thing.

I had to find a way out of there or I was going to die, and after dealing with this man this last week I doubted it would be quick or pretty.

43

Detective Kennedy

Lemuche was out of the office, checking on a lead from another case. I was sitting at my desk going through Addison's file again. My partner's phone rang, and since he was out I picked it up.

"This is Detective Kennedy," I greeted the caller.

"Hi, Ryan, this is Kenz from DFU. Is LeMuche there?"

DFU is our Digital Forensics Unit. Lemuche had them working on tracking our HookedUp mystery man down.

"No, but you can talk to me. Whatcha got, anything?"

"Yes and no," he said. "This guy is pretty sophisticated."

"What does that mean for us?" I asked, frowning.

"It means we're having trouble IDing him," he replied. "Whoever this guy is set up some serious walls."

"How does one do that?" I asked. I could navigate technology fairly easily, but I certainly wasn't a geek.

"So he created his profile on the site using a secure anonymous operating system, like Tails. What he does is run it from a USB stick, so it leaves no digital footprint."

"So there's no way you can track him?"

"We can uniquely identify users based on their browsers, extensions and stuff like that. But this guy took steps to prevent that."

This wasn't what I wanted to hear.

"So that's it?" I asked, disappointed.

"Pretty much. I mean, I can keep trying, but we have other cases stacked up."

"Thanks, Kenz, I appreciate it. If you think of any other way to ID him, please let me or Lemuche know."

I hung up and stared moodily at the phone.

I was pretty certain this was our guy, and had put a lot of hope in DFU, but it looked like that was a bust. It looked like I had only one other prospect – the hair I found. Lemuche dismissed it, but I haven't seen too many dogs with strands of hair that long or that blonde.

I'd returned to Addison's apartment and was able to retrieve several other strands of hair from her hairbrush, and sent them to the crime lab along with the one I lifted from Jondo's basement. However, I was looking at a several day turnaround so I didn't have the answers yet.

I sighed, returned to my computer and I poured over the pictures I'd taken at Max Jondo's house for the hundredth time. I felt I was missing something, but what?

44

Daddy

I finally pulled Addison out of the basement. Her body language told me she'd been cowed, but when she looked at me the shuttered defiance in her eyes told me otherwise. However, she behaved enough to let me guide her upstairs and into the bathtub.

God, she stank. Again.

I put her in the tub and washed her body and hair. I knew bathing her like I would wash a dog humiliated her, which is of course why I did it. I was going to tame this bitch or be forced to get rid of her, it was up to her now.

As I washed her back she winced under her breath. I admit it looked pretty bad, and there would certainly be scars, but she brought it on herself. Having to scramble to conceal and move everything before the cops arrived here was nerve racking, and I came as close to panicking as I ever have. That was all her fault, so she had to be punished for it. There wouldn't be a next time or she would pay much more dearly. While I washed her I made damned sure she knew it too.

She said nothing, made no reply, just stared mutely at the tiles.

I let her dry herself and put her robe back on, then led her to the kitchen and cuffed her to the table. I'd already put Cheryl there.

Addison didn't look at her, and Cheryl kept holding on her with her eyes, like she was silently begging Addison to look up, to forgive her. For what? Cheryl wasn't the one that gave her the beating, I was. Women were a mystery sometimes.

I cooked some eggs for all of us, and for once Addison ate everything on her plate and drank every drop of her orange juice. I guess sleeping in a cold basement drains your energy.

I was clearing the table when I heard a car slow down on the road outside and looked out of the kitchen window.

Fuck! Not again!

Seriously bad timing, but then again, it was beginning to seem it was never good timing for me around here anymore.

"Up, Cheryl! Right now!" I barked at her.

She immediately stood up, looking suddenly scared. I quickly uncuffed her, yanked open the basement door and shoved her toward the stairs.

"Down!"

She cast a terrified look at Addison but did what I said. I uncuffed Addison and yanked her up, squeezing her arm hard to remind her who was in charge here. I dragged her down the steps after Cheryl, who was now standing uncertainly at their base.

"On the mattress, Cheryl," I ordered.

She hesitated a moment, then obeyed me. I hauled Addison over to the cage, pulling both hands behind her and handcuffing them securely. I pulled a bandana from my pocket and shoved it in her mouth, then pulled the tie from her robe and bound it so she couldn't talk much less scream. I shoved her in the cage and locked it. She began kicking at the mesh immediately.

I leaned down and hissed, "Stay quiet or this will be your last memory on earth."

She stopped her kicking.

I then rushed over to Cheryl, cuffed her leg to the bolt in the wall, and said in a menacing voice, "One word out of your mouth and I'll come back down and bash your fucking head in."

Her eyes went wide and she nodded.

My asshole father was still sitting in his car when I went outside to prevent him coming inside.

He donned a fake smile and rolled his window down. "I was just about to come and knock on your door."

"Get the fuck out of here," I said through gritted teeth.

"Nice to see you, too," he replied wryly.

"I mean it —" I began, furious.

"I know, I know, you're busy," he said, cutting me off. "What else is new? You know what you need? A vacation. You spend too much damned time locked up in that house."

Just then I thought I heard a muffled scream. It was Addison, of course. But it was so muzzled and indistinct it didn't worry me.

"What was that?" my father asked, craning his heads toward the house.

"Nothing," I replied calmly.

"Funny, I thought I heard —"

"It's just the TV."

He snorted. "I'd hardly call that working hard," he sneered.

"What do you know about work? At least I pay my own bills," I said between my teeth.

"I pay my bills," he said, offended.

"With other people's money," I snapped at him.

He took a step toward me then, one hand closed in a tight fist.

"What? You gonna hit me, dad?" I asked scornfully.

He took a deep breath and relaxed his hand. He knew the pleasure it would give me to beat the shit out of him.

"Take a hike, dad, I got things to do." I turned from him and started for the house.

"Wait a second," he pleaded. "I… I really need to talk to you. Can we just go inside?"

"No," was all I replied, not stopping.

"I'm sick, son."

For Christ's sake! Another lie. Why couldn't he just leave me the fuck alone? I shook my head and started walking again.

"Prostate cancer!" He called after me. "Found out two days ago."

I finally stopped and swung around, glaring at him.

"You think I'm gonna cry for you? You been paying attention at all in this life?"

"I need more money," he said.

"Of course you do," I said.

"I can't help it if I got all these medical bills now."

"I don't care," I thrust. "Your problems are yours."

"I know you think you had a hard life," he retorted. "But the fact is you don't know what hard is."

"Try growing up in your house, with you and that bitch you married," I spat at him.

His face hardened. "Watch how you talk about your mother, boy."

I strode back. "She stopped being my mother a long time before she died, you worthless fuck! Remember that one beating that almost put her in the hospital? The time you saw a guy sneaking out of the house when you came home early?" I was seething now. "Well, he was just one in a long line of men. She deserved that beating." I thrust my face close to his and said in a low growl, "But you beat her for the wrong reason."

He looked honestly taken aback. "I don't know what you mean."

"Who do you think those guys were actually fucking? It wasn't her." I paused clenching and unclenching my fists. "How do you think she was able to afford to feed us and get booze for herself?"

He paled, his face suddenly ashen. "I… I didn't know," he whispered.

"I've been paying your way long enough. You come back here again and I'll kill you."

I turned and went back inside, slamming the door on him. I'd suffered enough because of that old piece of shit. If he had the nerve to come back I'd kill him, I really would. Wouldn't be the first time I've killed someone.

45

Addison

I heard the door upstairs bang open against the wall, then slam shut again. His feet pounded down the stairs and he strode in, his face was tight with rage, fury emanating from every pore. He stood there, looking back and forth between us, trying to decide which of us was going to bear the brunt of his wrath.

Cheryl cringed back against the wall.

I could see the moment he decided on me. His eyes narrowed and he walked slowly, like a dangerous animal, toward the cage I was imprisoned in. He was in such a state he almost swayed like a drunk man.

I swallowed a whimper. I couldn't take any more punishment from him, my back was still raw from the whipping he'd given me. My heart began to race, and it thumped savagely against my chest. Please, god, I prayed. Don't let him kill me….

Because I could see it in his eyes.

He yanked the cage door open; he hadn't bothered to lock it because my hands were cuffed behind me. He grabbed a handful of my hair and pulled me from the cage unceremoniously. A blunt end of the mesh caught on one of my cheeks and scratched it deeply. I could feel blood bead up. He flung me across the room, and I would've screamed if I hadn't been gagged.

He grabbed the cage with both hands and forcefully threw it at Cheryl, who shrieked shrilly while trying to duck. He stood a moment, his hands balled into tight fists, and looked wildly around the room. Then he fixed his eyes on me again.

My heart stopped.

He sprung toward me, grabbed me by the throat and shoved me onto my back. The cuffs imprisoning my hands dug into my back painfully. His hands began to squeeze mercilessly. I desperately wanted to fight, to claw at him, anything to stop the choking. I tried to call out from behind the gag, but only a desperate croak made its way past. Little spots appeared before my eyes, and I was weakening from lack of oxygen. I gradually became conscious of a voice screaming nearby, then I numbly realized it was Cheryl.

"Daddy! Daddy! Stop it! Please! You don't have to do this! Please! You don't want to do this!"

He just growled something under his breath and squeezed harder.

"Stop it! Now!" she yelled.

He glared at her, but the pressure on my throat lessened, then he let go of my throat. A fit of coughing fought against the gag, and I breathed desperately in through my nose.

He stood above me, looking at Cheryl for what seemed eternity, then leaned down and yanked me to a sitting position. He untied the belt and yanked the bandana from my mouth. I coughed until I thought I'd hack up a piece of my lungs, then I gasped for more air. I sucked it in in grateful gulps.

He grabbed one of my arms and dragged me along the floor over to the mattress where she sat. He released her from the bolt in the wall and secured my leg there instead, then unlocked the handcuffs.

"Get up," he barked at her.

She did so quickly.

He leaned down until his face was almost touching mine, and I turned weakly away.

"'Mommy' is *not* a safe word here," he hissed.

He yanked Cheryl to her feet and pulled her up the stairs after him. The door slammed shut again.

I was alone.

I heard him yelling at her upstairs until it faded. He must have taken her back to other bedroom.

I looked at the grey gloom of the basement and it mirrored my soul, drained of color and light, a barren landscape where anything of beauty was unknown, and hope couldn't take root much less survive. I felt numb inside, without the energy or desire to keep fighting.

Whoever had just driven up to the house was another missed opportunity. I sagged, realizing I wasn't going to make it. I'd been viciously pulled into this hell, slowly stripped of everything that was me, and I could feel myself becoming hollow inside. I realized at that moment that even if I managed to escape this nightmare, I'd never be able to find the woman I once was. She was irretrievably gone.

Maybe it would be better if he did kill me. Then all this would finally be over.

The sound of tiny claws began to quietly scrabble in the dark shadows of the far basement, but I no longer cared. I wanted to cry — but I had no more tears.

46

Barb

I get it that those dumbass cops had to go by protocol, and that their hands were tied by official red tape, but they were too fucking slow!

It had been SIX days now since Addison went missing. And their useless tech people couldn't track down that last guy Addy hooked up with. Were they stupid or just incompetent?

So I decided it was time for a little citizen detective work.

I called out of work and went into action. I drove to the police station and marched up to Sargeant Wycowski's desk. Didn't anybody else ever man that desk? Or did he work twenty-four-seven? He didn't strike me as Mr. Work-Ethic. He looked up, and I could see he recognized me and he frowned.

"Detectives Kennedy and Lemuche aren't in, ma'am," he said, trying to dismiss me from the get-go.

"Where are they?" I demanded.

He raised his eyebrows in surprise. "That's their business."

"Are they still trying to find Addison Clifton?"

"Ma'am," he began with forced patience, "They do not inform me about their business."

I put my hands on my hips and tapped my toes, giving him a hard look that had scared men before. "The house that that delivery dude heard screaming coming from, I need that address."

He gave me a funny look. "I can't give you that."

"Yes, you can and you will. Right now."

"That's police business, and I'm not allowed to give that kind of information out."

I smacked his desk, startling him. "I need that address."

"You're not getting it from me. Now if you'll please —"

"You give me that address or I'll report to your superiors that you hit on me while on the job, that you propositioned me in an extremely obscene way."

He eyed me up and down scornfully. The fat bastard obviously thought I wasn't the kind of woman a man would *want* to make a pass at. Not only was he being unhelpful, but now he was being rude.

Finally he said, "Nice try, but we have video cameras here at the front desk. You need to leave now."

Shit. I should've have thought of that. I took another tact.

"Look, Sargeant, do you have family? A wife? A girlfriend maybe?" I doubted the girlfriend bit, but you never knew.

"Look, you need to —"

"If someone you really cared suddenly went missing, you'd want to do everything you could to try and find them, wouldn't you?"

He sighed. "I don't want to have to call an officer in here, but I will."

I could tell he meant it. I frowned at him. "Thanks for nothing," I growled and left the station.

Outside, I stood on the busy sidewalk and thought carefully. I'd already asked Kennedy for the address and he said no, and that fat shit in there did too. How could I get my hands on it? Then I had a thought. I pulled out my phone and dialed.

"Officer Miller speaking."

"Hi, Luke," I greeted him. "It's Barb."

"I know," he said. He didn't sound particularly glad to hear from me.

What the fuck? When did I become such a pariah? I decided to let it pass.

"Do you think you could find something out for me?"

"Depends," he replied carefully.

I told him the address I wanted. He said no, which I sort of expected. So I asked if he could find out who the delivery guy was that reported the incident. He said no. I wheedled and threatened and kept at him until he finally agreed to try. After all, the name of the delivery person wasn't protected information, or at least I didn't think so.

I thanked him in my sweetest voice, and asked when we could get together again. We made a date for that evening, and I hoped he would have something for me.

Sometimes you just get lucky. Or rather, the policeman you're dating does.

We met at Dusty's at seven. When I walked into the crowded restaurant he was already there. He was sitting at a rickety table in the corner and I wound my way through the throng and joined him. He leaned over and gave me a kiss. God, he was cute. If I weren't on a mission at the moment I'd have grabbed his jacket and hauled him back to my place right then. However, I needed info more than sex at the moment.

He ordered me a beer and turned to me. "Scott Bushey."

I scrunched my face, confused. "Who?"

"Scott Bushey. The delivery driver. He works for UPS."

I whooped at the top of my lungs and threw my arms around his neck, causing half of the place to turn and look at me.

"Pipe down, will you," he whispered as a tired looking waitress set my beer down.

"You're the best!" I cried and drained a third of my beer. "How'd you get his name?" I asked.

"Don't ask. I'd get into trouble if anyone found out." He gave me a serious look. "And don't you go blabbing about it either. I could get fired."

"Don't worry," I said, waving his concern away.

He ordered two hot dogs, then he looked at me suspiciously. "Now that you have his name, what are planning to do with the information?"

I donned an innocent look. "Nothing, I just want to talk to him, that's all."

"Uh-huh." I could tell he didn't believe me — which, of course, he shouldn't. "Stay out of police business, Barb. Kennedy is a good detective, he doesn't need *your* help. And Lemuche is a bit of a loose cannon from what I've heard. You don't want him coming after you."

"I told you, I just want to talk to the guy," I reaffirmed.

We ate some great dogs and the best fries ever, then we went back to my place and had great sex. I know I said I didn't need sex right then, but it was already too late to call the UPS guy. So I figured I might as well as fill in the time until morning with something fun.

47

Daddy

I made a mistake I try to never do, and that's letting anyone penetrate my emotional shield. However, I let my father goad me and let painful memories intrude, so I overreacted with Addison and almost killed her. That would happen in due course, but not yet. And I certainly wouldn't do it in the house, too messy and too much clean-up. I'd made that mistake only once.

She was still in the basement. If nothing else, thirst and hunger should have brought her to heel by now.

I was finishing up some work that was frankly overdue, and was going to go down and haul her ass back upstairs, when I heard a car slow on the road in front of my house.

For Christ's sake! My place had suddenly become Grand Central fucking Station!

I got up and went to the window. It had stopped near the end of the drive, but I couldn't see who was behind the wheel.

I thought quickly. Cheryl was in the bedroom, and Addison was still chained in the basement. I decided I better head off whoever it was before they came up to the house.

Hoping it wasn't another police detective, I ambled casually down the driveway, trying to look as if I was merely going down to check the mail, for the box was near the stopped car. I was hoping the sight of me might startle them and they'd leave, but the car sat idling, like whoever it was waited for me. I didn't take that as a good sign. If it was the police I was truly fucked because, unlike the last time they showed up, I hadn't had any chance to conceal the girls or any evidence of them.

My heart was beating faster as I approached and bent down to see who was behind the wheel. It was a woman. I immediately relaxed. She certainly didn't look like she was affiliated with the police, if anything more like the opposite. She was on the plump side, with short, spiky red hair, and wore a leather jacket, despite the warm day. She looked like she was a member of a biker gang.

I motioned for her to roll down the passenger window, which she did. She just stared at me, and I had to admit it was unsettling.

"Can I help you?" I asked in a pleasant voice. "Are you looking for someone?"

She snorted and replied, "Yeah, I am."

"Where are you trying to get to?"

She studied my face intently, her own unreadable. She was beginning to make me uncomfortable.

"I'm looking for a friend."

I smiled. "Well, I'm sorry, but there aren't any houses anywhere near here for miles, I don't usually even see much traffic along this road. She certainly doesn't live anywhere nearby. You probably made a wrong turn somewhere."

When I wanted to I could be extremely charming. Most woman instantly fell under my spell when I exerted myself. However, I could see she wasn't falling for it, and I got another uncomfortable itch on the back of my neck.

"Oh, yeah?" she asked, her eyes narrowing. "That's not what my GPS said."

"Um… sorry, but yeah. Looks like it must've got it wrong."

"So there's nobody in that house but you?" she asked, clipping her words for emphasis.

What the fuck?

My own eyes narrowed at her, matching her suspicion. "What do you want?" I asked tersely.

"I want my friend," she replied, never taking her eyes from mine.

I didn't like where this bullshit was going. "I already told you you've made a mistake," I said gruffly, "I think you'd better move on."

For the first time she turned her gaze past me at the house. She studied it long and hard, then instead of driving forward, she put her car in neutral and opened her door.

I looked quickly up and down the long rural road and slid my hand back to the gun I had wedged in the back of my jeans. I smiled. She wouldn't be the first stupid woman who'd underestimated me. The dense woods across the road already held several unmarked graves.

She got out and walked around the car to come face to face with me.

Definitely a stupid woman.

48

Barb

There was something off about the guy, I could feel it. Something about his eyes, the way he stood alert, like an animal waiting to pounce. Was he the guy who took my friend? I didn't know, but he made the little hairs on the back of my neck stand up.

A voice in my head told me to get back in my car and high-tail it the hell outta there, but my stubbornness got the better of me.

I needed to get a look inside the house, to see if there was evidence of Addison being held there, but I didn't know how to do it without acting suspicious or tipping him off.

Or getting hurt.

He stood there, watching me as I approached him, a strange small smile flickering on his lips. As I stopped a few feet away, I noticed he had one hand behind his back. An alarm bell rang in my head. Could he be hiding something? A knife, or maybe one of those stun guns? Luke tried to give me one of those once and I told him I was just fine without one, but suddenly I really wished I had one.

I backed up a step. “Um… Look, I didn’t mean to sound rude,” I said in a friendlier voice. I *really* wanted to get a look inside. “You’re probably right, I must’ve made a mistake. Maybe I got her address wrong.”

My change in attitude caused him to relax a little.

“No problem,” he replied in a force of politeness. “Like I said, it’s remote out here, I’m the only place for miles.”

“Here’s the thing, though,” I began apologetically, “I’m a little embarrassed but… I really, really gotta pee. Could I possibly use your bathroom?”

He seemed taken aback by my request, but almost immediately his face was stony. He shook his head. “Sorry, I don’t let strangers in my house.”

“Pleeease,” I said, putting a little frantic whine in there for effect. “I’m a little desperate at the moment.”

His eyes narrowed as he studied my face, then that strange little smile reappeared. Finally he said, “Well, I’d hate to turn my back on a lady in need.”

He stepped back and gestured for me to proceed him up the walk.

Suddenly the very advice I’d urged upon Addison echoed in my head.

Someone should always know where you are.

Luke knew I was trying to get this address, and could probably guess I’d worm it out of the UPS guy, but he’d warned me to stay out of police business, so I hadn’t told him I was coming today. I could walk inside that house and never be heard of again.

I’m stubborn, but I’m not stupid.

I suddenly stepped back. “You know, I think… I think I’ve changed my mind. I’ve already taken up enough of your time. I’m just gonna have to hold it. I’m sorry, I’ll just go.”

I turned and trotted around the car, trying to keep myself from full out running. I got in and shut the door, instantly locking every door. I waved, put the car in drive and slowly pulled away. I looked back at him in my rearview mirror.

He was standing where I'd left him, watching me intently.

Very creepy.

At that moment I truly hoped he wasn't the guy who took Addison, because if he were I didn't think she'd have a chance in hell, and in fact might already be dead.

Please don't let it be him, I prayed devoutly as he finally disappeared behind me.

49

Daddy

That bitch was lucky she had a little more room left in her bladder.

50

Detective Kennedy

Lemuche and I were on our way back to the station after looking into a case of elder abuse. Despite having a search warrant the man's daughter tried to refuse us entry. It got pretty contentious, and Lemuche ended up having to subdue the woman. It was a pretty bad scene inside once we got past her. With some of the things I've seen, I'm sometimes surprised I haven't become an alcoholic. Enough cops are, and for good reason. We've seen shit most people would never dream of.

We were almost at the station when my phone rang. I looked at the caller ID, Barbara Meade. Again. I was going to decline the call then sighed and changed my mind. I knew she'd just keep calling.

"Hello, Ms. Meade."

"Detective Kennedy, you need to go back to 1906 Wright Rd.! I'm sure that was the guy that kidnapped Addison," she said in a rush.

"We've already been there," I replied patiently.

I know the woman was getting on Lemuche's nerves, but I could understand her panic in a situation like this. However, it was my job to try and keep her calm.

"There was nothing.... How did *you* find that address?" I suddenly wanted to know.

"Well, I just left there," she replied, ignoring my question. "And he creeped me the fuck out! He's hiding something, I'm sure of it."

I looked at the phone in consternation. "What were you doing there?" I repeated sharply.

Lemuche looked over at me. "Where?"

"Max Jondo's house," I answered him.

"How in the hell did she get the address?" he asked, an edge to his voice.

I shrugged and returned to Ms. Meade. "You need to stay out of this and let us handle it," I said sternly.

"But you aren't handling it!" she almost shrieked at me. "If you guys were doing your fucking job she'd be found by now!"

"Tell her to stop calling, and you stop talking to her," Lemuche said to me. "She's meddling now, and getting in the way. Tell her we'll arrest her for interference if she doesn't stop."

I ignored him. "Ms. Meade, I understand you're worried but we're doing all we can at the moment. Now stay away from that man's house, do you understand me?"

She didn't answer, but I could hear her breathing heavily on the other end.

"Ms. Meade?"

"Fine!" she finally huffed. "But you need to go back there. There's something wrong with that man."

"That may be, but he has no direct bearing on your missing friend," I replied.

"She has a fucking name, Detective."

She hung up on me.

I sighed and slipped my phone back into my jacket pocket.

She thought I was depersonalizing Addison Clifton. Nothing was further from the truth.

Of all the cases I deal with, and that includes homicides, I hate missing persons the most. I hate seeing the frantic worry in their relatives eyes, I hate the thought that we might never find them, never know what happened to them. I always try to put myself in the shoes of those families who are out of their minds with anxiety. It's the not knowing that drives you insane, so people tend to imagine the absolute worse things. Unfortunately, that doesn't make my job any easier.

"What was that woman doing there?" Lemuche asked angrily.

"I don't know, but she obviously talked to Jondo. She said he creeped her out," I replied.

He snorted. "More likely the other way around. You've seen her."

I smiled a little. "Yeah. But she's scared."

"Tough shit," he said. "That doesn't mean she can meddle with our case. If you don't tell her to back off, I will."

I looked at him. He was behind the wheel, and I could see a small vein thrumming in the side of his forehead. I knew why he was upset, but she certainly wasn't the first person to try to *help* the police.

"I think she will," I said calmly, but I privately agreed with him. Civilians trying to aid the police usually caused more problems for us.

Of course, Lemuche's responses to things were always a little unpredictable. More time on the job would mellow him — that, or get him kicked out of the force — it just depended on which way he chose to go.

"Anyway," he continued, "I think we're too late on this one."

"What do you mean?" I asked.

He shrugged. "You know how it goes, Ryan. It's been a week since she went missing. Gotta get them in the first seventy-two hours. Hate to say it, but the woman's probably already dead."

He was right about the timeline with a missing person, but something nagged me about this one, something told me she was still out there and not dead yet.

"Maybe," I finally said. "But if that's the case, I want to find her body and put the asshole that made her that way out of commission for good."

He nodded and grinned. "My kind of partner."

We spent the rest of the afternoon writing reports, and at five o'clock I stood and stretched.

"You heading out?" I asked Lemuche.

He sat back and scratched his head. "Nah, I think I'm going to go through a few files here."

"Addison Clifton?"

He quirked an eyebrow at me. "Go home, I'll see you in the morning."

I nodded and walked away. As I got into my car I wondered if he was right. I really hoped he wasn't.

51

Addison

I had always embraced solitude, but this was more than I could take. I'd been alone in the basement for hours on end.

Well, I guess I wasn't really alone. There was the rat. Although I hadn't seen him again, I could still sometimes hear him scrabbling about in the dim recesses of the large dark room.

Also, *he* came down once. Thankfully, he didn't touch me, he was only there to bring me food and water. He never spoke a word to me while there, and I refused to even look at him.

My throat still hurt but it was starting to be a little less painful to swallow, and even the horrible stinging of my back had ebbed. It was a low throb now, but it had started to itch, and I was going crazy because I couldn't reach to scratch it in places.

My emotional state was falling rapidly into a dark well of misery. That hollow feeling I'd been carrying was turning to total apathy. I'd always been a fighter, I'd always been tenacious and stubborn, but now I had gotten to the point where I truly just didn't care about anything anymore.

Since my captivity, I spent the time I'd been left alone recalling Matt and Justin. I pictured every detail of their faces, every gesture, every nuance of their voices. I saw the errant lock of hair that always fell onto Matt's forehead, the way he stroked my face after we made love. I heard the high peals of laughter from my son, Justin, and could literally remember the smell of his young skin, the feel of his arms around my neck in one of our many hugs. But I refused to allow myself to do that anymore. It hurt too much. It was also a stark reminder of how far I'd sunk.

I'd also spent a great deal of time plotting how to escape, but the two times I'd had any kind of chance I'd been thwarted. Even my fantasies of killing *Daddy* weren't enough anymore.

I no longer cared if he lived or died. I just wanted him far away from me, and me far away from this house. But now I believed that would probably never happen. I was going to die here. Part of me felt it would be a relief.

Exhausted, I watched a laser thin beam of light that had snuck in through the high window as it slowly travelled across the floor, wishing I could be outside in the sunlight again, to feel its warmth on my skin, soaking into every pore.

Late in the afternoon he came down, immediately undid his pants and threw me onto my belly, taking me forcefully from behind. My ankle was still cuffed to the chain in the wall, but I stretched an arm toward the thin ray of light streaking the cold floor in front of me. It was just out of my reach. Suddenly I was desperate to touch it, and the thought of it overshadowed the reality of what was being done to me at that moment. I stretched my arm to its limit, but the tips of my fingers couldn't quite touch it.

He wasn't gentle and when he at last breathed that grunt of satisfaction and withdrew from me, I barely noticed, I was so obsessed with that light, which was now slowly drawing away from me again. I wanted to cry out for it to come back, not to leave me alone in that dank basement. I felt something wet on my cheek, and I realized with small surprise it was a tear. I thought I had run out of tears.

Without saying anything, he stood up behind me. I didn't bother to look back, but I heard him zipping his pants and the stairs creaking under his weight as he left. I sat up and leaned back against the wall, still staring longingly toward the slip of light snaking away from me.

I wiped the tears away. I could tell my face was grubby but I didn't care. I glanced to the right — and froze.

His cell phone was lying on the edge of the mattress!

It must've fallen out of his pocket when he dropped his pants, and he never noticed it before leaving.

Oh, my god, I couldn't believe it!

I lunged for it and feverishly dialed 911 with hands that shook so badly I almost didn't get the numbers right.

"What's your emergency?" asked the voice on the other end.

"Thank god!" I whispered urgently. "My name's Addison Clifton. I was kidnapped and have been held captive at 1906…," I paused, frantically trying to remember the address on the package. "I… I think it's Wright Street, in Trouville." Please god, let me be right! I prayed I wasn't remembering it wrong. "I'm in the basement. Please send someone here right away!"

"I'm contacting the police department right now. Please stay on the line with me, ma'am," the dispatcher said.

I heard footsteps overhead.

"I can't!" I whispered. "I have to hang up. Send someone immediately."

I ended the call. Then I went to recent calls, deleting the 911 call as quickly as my trembling fingers allowed, and shoved the phone half under the mattress, hoping it would look as if it had fallen and gone unnoticed by me. I heard the basement door being flung open and flopped down, desperately trying to still my rapid heartbeat and look as if I was exhausted and resigned.

He came rushing down the stairs and stopped at the foot of the mattress. I didn't look up but I could feel his stare burning into me.

"Where is it?" he growled between closed teeth.

I turned my head listlessly and gave him a blank look.

"What the fuck did you do?" he demanded.

I just looked at him with fake incomprehension.

He knelt down and clutched my throat, squeezing, as he thrust his face into mine.

"Where — is — it?"

I shook my head, widening my eyes. He stared at me for a long moment, then he let go and began searching the area. Finally, he spied the phone and made a fast grab for it.

I gasped, hoping I'd created the right mix of surprise and disappointment, like I'd been unaware of its existence and it was yet another missed opportunity for escape. I tried to look crushed, which in my present state wasn't hard.

He turned it on and searched it, then seemed to relax. He threw me a suspicious look but he no longer seemed to have the frantic urgency he did a moment ago. Unexpectedly, he reached over and unlocked the cuff, freeing me.

"Get up," he commanded.

I tried to do so but stumbled in the process; my legs were weak beneath me. He took hold of my arm and yanked me upright.

"Up the stairs," he said. "I'm not going to carry you."

He had me precede him, holding my arm in a tight grip the entire way upstairs. My eyes blinked in the sudden light.

He marched me to the bedroom I'd occupied earlier and thrust me inside. He left, but only for a moment. He returned with Cheryl, pushed her inside and closed the door after her.

I heard his phone ringing in the hallway, and I prayed it wasn't 911 calling the phone back. Then I heard him answer. "Hey, Buddy-boy." His voice faded as he walked away from the room.

"Are… are you okay?" Cheryl asked me timidly.

I smiled.

52

Daddy

I just heard it across the wire, you got another cop on the way."

My heart began to race off the chart.

"What the fuck?" I asked, stunned. "I thought that was all taken care of! Why is he coming back here?"

"Not the same guy, Max. It's a marked unit. They're answering a 911 call."

Shit. I thought about the woman who stopped in front of the house earlier. Did she suspect something? She was certainly acting weird. Did that bitch call the cops on me?

"Thanks for the heads up," I said.

I was about to hang up when he said in a rush, "Max! You don't have the lead time you did before."

"Okay." I started thinking feverishly about what to do.

"And Max? The call came from your house."

He hung up and I stared at the phone in my hand.

That bitch. That fucking bitch!

She had just used up the small amount of goodwill I had left toward her. She'd been a good lay, but she was fucking done.

I raced into the kitchen and out the door to the garage. Like before I started the car up, threw open the hood and turned the radio on loud. It boomed through the small space.

I was just in time. I heard a car pull into my drive and peeked around the hood. It was a police car. It stopped midway up the drive, a cop got out and approached the garage where I was. I noted his hand hovered near his holstered gun. I had left mine back in my desk. Shit. But I really hadn't had the time to retrieve it anyway. However, I had made a hasty backup plan.

"Sir," the cop called out to me.

I chose not to hear him.

"Sir! Sir!" he yelled out.

I pretended to be startled and looked around the hood at him. "Shit!" I called. "Sorry, you startled me, officer."

"Can you please turn the car and the radio off? Now, sir."

I nodded and rushed around to comply. I reached through the driver's window and switched everything off again. I noted what was sitting on the driver's seat and tried not to smile. Even when I was under the gun I was genius at last minute inventiveness. I wiped my sweaty palm nervously on my pants for his benefit.

"How can I help you, Officer?" I said.

"We got a 911 call from this house," he replied seriously, keeping his eyes firmly fixed on me.

"From my house?" I asked in utter astonishment.

"Yes, sir. Are you Max Jondo?"

"Yes. But… I don't understand. I'm the only one here, and I never made a 911 call. Are you sure you got the right address?"

"Quite sure."

“But I’m telling you, it couldn’t have come from here. I don’t even have a land line. I mean, who does these days, right?” I added a small laugh for effect.

“The call was made from a cell phone registered in your name, Mr. Jondo,” he said.

“That could be,” I replied.

“So you admit it came from your phone?”

“Well, I don’t know for sure. You see, I lost my phone yesterday. I’m not sure where. I was out running errands, and when I got home I realized it was gone. So anybody could’ve found it and used it. Sounds like a prank to me.”

“Uh-huh.”

I couldn’t tell if he was buying it or not.

53

Addison

I was caught in the grip of excitement. I rushed forward and grabbed Cheryl's arm.

"We're about to be rescued," I said in a rush.

She gave me a funny look, tilted her head and asked in a confused voice, "What're you talking about?"

I tiptoed to the door and put my head against it, listening to see if I could hear him anywhere near. As far as I could tell he wasn't. I darted back to Cheryl.

"I called 911 and gave them this address!" I whispered excitedly.

"You what?" Her eyes grew huge. "How?"

"He accidentally dropped his phone in the basement. He never even noticed, so when he went back upstairs I called them."

She looked absolutely stunned. "W-what did they say?"

"I had to hang up and erase the call. And I was just in time, too. He came storming back down to get it, and I pretended I hadn't seen it. He seemed to buy it, so he brought me back here."

"Yes, but… wow." She looked around, as if bewildered.

"Isn't that great news?" I said excitedly, grabbing her arm again.

"Of course! Absolutely! I just… I guess I'm so surprised I don't know how to take it all in. After all this time…." She stopped, grew thoughtful and worried looking. "Hey, Addison, what if he does the same thing he did last time the police showed up here? Then we'll still be stuck, but it'll be even worse. Remember what he did to you after that, he almost tore your back to ribbons. Do you want that to happen again? Next time he might even kill you. Maybe me, too. I'm sorry, but it scares me."

I wanted to scream. She was right, but she was wrong, too. If we never took a chance, we'd both die here.

I thought I heard something outside. "Shh! Hold on a sec."

I rushed to the shuttered window. I couldn't really see much but I listened as hard as I could. Then I heard it, a car engine was starting up. I turned to Cheryl, feeling exultant.

"I think that's his car. He's leaving for the first time without chaining us down! Now's our chance."

"Chance for what?"

"To break out of here," I cried.

"Shouldn't we just wait for the police to show up?"

"No."

She looked at me, confusion all over her face. "No?"

"If he's not here when they come, they may not try to force their way inside the house. They'd need a warrant for that anyway. If we could get out of this room, we could already be outside when they show up," I replied, thinking feverishly. I know I was being crazy, but I was so desperate to get out of there I was being illogical.

She shook her head. "Sorry, I'm not following you. How're we supposed to do that? The door's locked, and it's too strong to break.

Anyway, you said you heard his car start, so if he's not here we could just scream or something when we hear them pull up."

That wasn't enough for me anymore. I couldn't wait because we probably wouldn't have this opportunity again. I looked all around the room, trying to rack my brain for a way to escape. My eyes lighted on one of the electrical plates near the baseboard, and I let them travel up the wall's surface. I rushed over to it, it was the wall that separated our two bedrooms, and I began knocking on it every few inches.

"What're you doing?" she wanted to know.

"You're right," I replied, "We can't break down the door. Believe me, I've tried." I turned to her, excited with my idea. "But the walls!" I turned back and continued knocking, listening for where the studs might be. "They're just two sheets of drywall. It's hollow in between."

"So?" she asked, confused.

"So maybe the door in your room isn't locked!"

I pushed the bed out of the way and sat down on the floor, facing the wall.

"My boss always said I never thought out of the box. Maybe she was right," I continued, then looked over my shoulder at Cheryl and grinned. "But like you said before, some situations change things."

I kicked as hard as I could. My foot went right through the drywall.

"Holy shit!" cried Cheryl, and she rushed over, looking at the new hole in amazement.

I kicked several more times and soon had a sizeable hole. I kept at it and soon the opening was nearly two feet wide. I pulled myself closer so I could get at the other side. One big punch and I had a small hole. I looked at Cheryl triumphantly.

"That son-of-a-bitch has touched me for the last time!"

I continued to violently kick at the further wall.

"Addison!" called Cheryl.

I stopped and looked her. "What?"

"You're bleeding. Your foot."

I looked and saw blood trickling down my right ankle. It must've been grazed by the rough edges of the broken drywall, which hung down in strips like broken teeth.

"It's not bad," I replied, brushing it away.

"Do you want me to kick for a while so you can tend to it?" she asked.

"I'm done. It's big enough for us to squeeze through already."

She eyed the small jagged holes dubiously. Then I heard her chuckle behind me.

"What?" I asked.

"I could almost read your mind," she answered. "Every kick was making you feel better, wasn't it? We call it Destructive therapy, where smashing things in a controlled environment relieves stress and anxiety."

"You know what I call it, Cheryl?"

"What?"

"The road to freedom."

I looked up at her with shining eyes.

"Let's get out of here."

I rose to my knees and pushed myself through the opening sideways, using my right arm to steady me on the other side. My hips almost got stuck on the further side, but I forced my passage, tearing some more of the wall. I finally made it to the other side and looked back at her through the opening.

"Your turn."

She was a little larger than me and she struggled to get through the opening, but the drywall continued to fall apart and she finally got through. I helped her to stand and we held each other for a moment, laughing.

I broke from her and headed for the door.

"We're almost there," I said in a whisper.

I held my breath and turned the knob. I almost cried with relief when it clicked. I eased the door open and looked; the hallway was empty. Cheryl pulled me back, and I looked at her, surprised.

"I know the place better than you," she said. "Follow me."

"Let's just run out the front door," I argued. "And keep running."

"Do you want to get caught?" she demanded.

"Of course not. But we heard him leave."

She shook her head. "We don't know that for sure. Follow me."

She slipped through the door and I followed. She ran quietly down the hall, then she stopped and waved me forward.

"A lot of places have cameras at their front doors now. If he has one, we'll get caught on it and it'll alert his phone."

I hadn't thought of that. She was right.

"Let's go to the kitchen," she continued, "One of the doors leads to the garage. If he's still around or fairly close by, there's less chance of us being seen that way. We can find a place to hide until the cops get here."

I nodded, and she darted toward the kitchen, me on her heels. Once inside she went straight to a side door. She paused, looking back at me for a moment, then turned the knob and very slowly eased it open a crack. She immediately shut it again.

"What's wrong?" I whispered urgently.

"His car's still out there, he didn't leave at all," she whispered back. "We are so fucked, Addison."

"Shit."

54

Daddy

The cop wasn't buying my story.

"I need to check inside your house, sir," he said, his hand still hovering beside his holster.

Shit.

"Do you have a warrant?" I demanded.

There was a sudden noise from just inside the kitchen, it sounded like a chair had been knocked over. The cop looked quickly from me to the house and back to me again.

"I thought you said —" he began.

"My dog," I said quickly, cutting him off.

"Please step aside, sir."

I had no choice now.

He stepped toward the door that led to the kitchen. The minute his back was turned I reached through the open window of my car and my hand closed tightly around the tire iron I'd put there earlier.

I struck his head with full force, and he fell limply to the ground. But I had to be sure. I hit him three more times to make sure he wouldn't get up again. Blood pooled around his battered head.

I was about to rush inside when — for fuck's sake! — another car pulled into my drive.

I looked up in a complete panic.

55

Addison

Cheryl stood frozen next to the chair she'd accidentally knocked over, her eyes wide with fear. I rushed over and grabbed her arm.

"Pull yourself together," I hissed as quietly as I could.

"I'm so sorry, Addison," she breathed.

I looked over her shoulder, panicked he might have heard us. "Let's just get the hell out of here," I whispered frantically, and began to pull her away.

Then of all the stupid things, Cheryl started crying.

I wanted to slap her, we didn't have time for hysterics. I tugged but she seemed rooted to the spot. My heart was beating a mile a minute, and I was terrified that any minute he would walk through that door. I stood still, straining to listen for him. I wanted to run, but there was no way I was going to leave her behind, not after everything we'd been through together. I suddenly reached over and shook her by her shoulders.

"Please, Cheryl," I implored her. "Let's get to the front door. We'll have to chance a camera. We can't let him find us. Please!"

She gave me a dazed look, then finally swallowed and nodded. I released her.

"Come on," I whispered under my breath. "But for god's sake be quiet."

We tiptoed out of the kitchen again and dashed as silently as we could across the living room. I fumbled with the dead bolt for what felt like forever, then finally I managed to get it unlocked. I looked over at her. She was watching me, her eyes huge.

"We can do this," I whispered. I eased the door open. "Let's go."

56

Daddy

The new arrival stopped and parked behind the police car. The door opened and Detective Lemuche got out.

He saw me before I could move, so I stood there and waited for him, gripping the tire iron tightly. I watched as he slid one hand inside his coat jacket, probably going for his concealed weapon. I broke out in a sweat.

I was in for some very serious shit.

"Where's the officer?" Lemuche called, looking carefully around, trying to spot him.

I cleared my throat but I didn't answer. What was there to say?

By the time he cleared the marked car and stepped into the garage, he already had his gun out. He glanced down and saw the dead cop on the ground, his head a battered mess, lying in a spreading pool of blood.

Lemuche stared at him for a long time, shocked, then slowly raised his eyes and fixed them on me. His jaw tightened and so did his grip on his gun.

"I think we have a big problem here," he said with an edge to his voice.

I held up my free hand. "I can explain," I said nervously.

"No," he replied angrily, "I don't think so. You killed a cop. You'll get life." He glared at me. "If you live that long."

Believe it or not, another car driving down the street slowed and chose that moment to pull into my drive. Jesus fucking Christ!

I immediately recognized the old beat up vehicle.

I go weeks, months without seeing a goddamned soul on this street, now suddenly every fucking person in the world decides to pay me a visit all at once.

"Jesus!" I breathed.

Lemuche backed up so he could check out the newcomer.

The door opened and my father got out of the car.

"I gotta keep him away," I said without thinking, and I darted forward to intercept him. Lemuche put a strong hand on my arm and stopped me.

"Step back," he said.

"But—"

"I said, step back," he reiterated. "Don't move."

We watched as the old man ambled slowly up the drive. He continued until he spied the cop car, stopped and frowned at it, then looked over at me and Lemuche.

"What's wrong?" he called. "Are you in trouble?"

"Go home!" I called back.

He ignored me and hobbled around the car, continuing toward us. "What did you do now?" he asked as he stepped into the garage. Then he saw the bloody body lying on the ground and stopped abruptly, as though he had just been hit in the face.

"Holy shit," he whispered, obviously shocked to his core. He looked up at me with eyes so wide with amazement it was almost comical. Almost.

"Jesus, son!" he said. "What happened?" Then he spied Lemuche and stepped back, startled.

"You know," replied Lemuche, "You always did have lousy timing, *dad*."

He shot him square in the chest.

"What — the — fuck?" I cried, so surprised it felt like my heart stopped for moment.

He walked over and nudged our father's limp body. Blood was trickling out from under him, a rivulet that snaked its way to join the larger pool of the dead cop's. Eddie returned his gun to his holster and looked at me calmly.

"You think that piece of shit would've kept his mouth shut about this? He'd have used it to squeeze every nickel out of you. I'm helping you, Max," he said harshly.

"By shooting him?" I demanded.

I mean, it had been in my mind for some time to take out my dad, but the timing was ludicrous. Now we had two dead bodies to dispose of!

He stepped over the blood and thrust his face in mine. "I don't think you get it yet. You're in a world of trouble here. You killed a *cop*. What in the hell were you thinking?"

I was starting to get angry. "I didn't have a fucking choice. He was going into the house. I had to stop him or he would've found the women."

He turned away and looked out of the garage, thinking hard. Suddenly his shoulders became rigid.

"You mean those women?" he asked, whipping his head to look at me while pointing at something outside.

I stepped forward to get a better look at what he was talking about. I saw it almost immediately.

Addison and Cheryl were nearing the road, running straight for the thick line of trees beyond.

"Oh, fucking shit!"

I dashed out of the garage and started pumping my legs furiously after them. I could hear Buddy-boy right behind me. When I got my hands on her…!

57

Addison

We made it! We were finally out of that house!

I started running across the grass toward the road. For the first time I could see where we were. We were literally out in the middle of nowhere. His house was situated at the top of a hill, and from either side there was nothing but steep grades that led to empty countryside as far as the eye could see. A narrow two lane road wound in front of the house and disappeared down the hill in each direction. Across the road was a vast wooded area that looked as if it stretched for miles.

There were two cars in the driveway, and one of them was a police car! I stopped, grabbing Cheryl.

"Look!" I whispered. "It's the police. Thank god! They must have been sent by 911."

She took hold of my arm, stopping me from dashing over to it. "No!" she wailed. "It could be his half-brother, *he's* a cop, and believe me, you don't want to meet him. If anything, he's even worse than Daddy," she said, obviously scared to death.

"But 911 said they were sending the police, it has to be them!"

"But what if it isn't?" she asked, her voice betraying her panic. "Buddy-boy could have intercepted the call. He's helped Daddy before like that. What if it's him and they're just waiting for us to run right into their arms? You know what kind of consequences we'd be in for. Please, Addison! I'm scared. Let's just keep running. Let's just get as far away from this place as fast we can."

I wasn't sure what to do. We desperately needed help, but if she was right he'd kill us. I knew I was wasting time trying to decide, but I was torn. Cheryl took the decision out of my hands by running across the huge expanse of lawn toward the road. I followed and soon passed her.

I heard her breath coming out in harsh rasps. I slowed for her to catch up, and grabbed her arm to help her move faster. There was no way I was going to let this opportunity fail like the last two. We had to move, and fast.

"I… I don't know if I can…," Cheryl gasped beside me.

I clutched her arm tighter and ran even faster. "Yes, you can," I encouraged. "Let's head for the trees, there's cover there."

I heard a car and we both stopped as one.

"Let's flag them down and see if they'll give us a ride," I said, excitedly.

Cheryl grabbed my arm and squeezed. "There's hardly ever any traffic here. If someone is heading this way they're close with Daddy, or at least know him. That would be the end of us, Addison."

That made me pause.

We stood uncertainly, unsure if it was someone who would help or who might hinder our escape. I didn't want to take a chance on failure, not when we were so close. We had to cross the road to get to the trees, and whoever was in the car would see us. My heart thumped wildly, and my head whipped in all directions, looking for a place we could hide. Cheryl made the decision for me when she dropped to the ground, dragging me down with her.

"Lay flat and stay still!" she hissed under her breath.

Since I was already down I really didn't have any choice. We listened as the car topped the hill. I decided if it passed us, we'd get up and chase it down, calling for help. But it didn't. We listened as it slowed then pulled into the driveway to our right and stopped.

We listened as the door opened and an older man called out, "What's wrong? Are you in trouble?"

It looked like Cheryl was right. Thank god I didn't flag him down. We still had to keep our heads about us, there were still too many traps we could step into. Until we were far away, we couldn't afford to make any mistakes.

"Go home!"

I cringed. It was *him*. Even the sound of his voice caused a shiver to trip down my spine.

I raised my head very slightly and watched as an old man wound his way past the parked cars and entered the garage. I turned to Cheryl.

"Let's go. *Now*!" I whispered fiercely.

She grabbed my shoulder and shook her head wildly. "What if—?"

A shot rang out, echoing inside the garage walls.

I didn't waste any more breath, just scrambled up as fast as I could, pulling her up with me. We made a mad dash for the road. We hit the pavement in our bare feet and headed for the trees.

Suddenly, I heard a shout, followed by the sound of feet pounding on the grass behind us. We'd been seen!

"Run! Run! Run!" I cried to Cheryl breathlessly with surging panic, my heart feeling like it would explode from my chest any minute.

If we could just make it to the trees, I knew we might be able to at least find a place to hide. I ran as if my life depended on it — which it did.

58

Barb

Luke was off duty at five, so I called him and told him he had to come over to my apartment immediately. He tried to make excuses so I threatened to go to his place and start screaming his name at the top of my lungs. He said he'd come.

He finally arrived around six-thirty.

"What took you so damn long?" I demanded.

He shrugged. "I had to change outta my uniform, and a couple of the guys asked me to join them for a beer, so I did."

"You went drinking?" I almost shouted at him.

"Yeah. What's the big deal, Barb?"

"The big deal is that I need you."

He grinned lasciviously and grabbed me around the waist. "Feeling horny, honey?"

I wriggled out of his grasp and pushed him away. “No,” I said irritably. “I don’t need you that way.”

He scrunched up his face in confusion. “Then what do you want?”

“I want you to go somewhere with me,” I replied.

“Okay,” he said, then gave me a suspicious look. “Where?”

I pulled up my map app on my phone and tapped on a stored address then showed it to him. “There.”

“He looked at it and frowned. “Where’s that?”

“It’s the house Scott Bushey told me about.”

“Who’s Scott Bushey?” he asked.

“He’s the delivery man whose name you gave me. The one that heard a woman screaming inside this house,” I replied.

He crossed his arms and gave me a stern look. “I told you to stay out of police business.”

“So did Detective Kennedy, but that didn’t stop me from going out there yesterday afternoon,” I said, raising my chin defiantly.

“You did WHAT? I told you — !“ he yelled.

“I don’t give a shit what you or that detective told me!” I yelled back. “I want to find my best friend!”

“Not only are you meddling in a missing person case, but if that guy *is* keeping her, it was dangerous as hell. What a crazy stunt. That’s the most idiotic thing you’ve ever done — and you’ve done some stupid things, Barb.”

“I know, I know,” I said. “I have to admit, the guy seemed really sketchy to me.”

“Oh, Jesus, you actually talked to the guy that lives there?”

I started to pace my living room and told him the story of what happened, and how I got the willies at the last minute and didn’t go in.

“Well, at least you did one smart thing,” he said. “So that’s why you got me here, to take you back there?”

"Yes," I replied. "If you were with me I'd feel safer trying to catch him off guard, maybe trap him into saying something about Addison."

"No," he said quickly.

"But Luke —!"

He took me by the arm and made me look into his face. He said, "If I did something like that I could get kicked off the force. I can't jeopardize my job like that."

I understood, I really did, but I was feeling desperate by then. I thought quickly, and then I came up with an idea.

"Okay, I get it. So follow me in your own car instead."

He raised his eyebrows. "How is that any better, Barb?"

"Look, if anyone finds out, you can just say you didn't trust me —"

"That's not a stretch."

"And you followed me to make sure I wasn't going to get into any trouble, or, as you put it, that I wouldn't meddle with the case. That keeps you from being an abettor, or whatever they're called."

"Barb…," he said with a long sigh.

"Pleeaase."

"No."

I crossed my arms and gave him a hard look. "You can either follow me or I'll go by myself. AND I'll tell Kennedy that you were the one that gave me the delivery guy's name."

His mouth fell open.

59

Detective Kennedy

I'd only been home a short time when my phone rang. I looked at the caller ID, and I was surprised to see is was from the digital forensics unit. I answered.

"Hey, Detective Kennedy, it's Kenz again."

"Hi, Kenz. What's up? Anything new on the Clifton case?"

"Yeah, I think we found your guy."

I sat up straighter and set my beer down. "You're kidding! I thought you said he was untraceable."

"Yeah, but I hate unsolved mysteries, so I kept at it during my down time between other cases. It took a while, but I kept going back in time until I found an early profile of his. Bingo! He didn't have the same level of sophistication on that one. The site's tracking script was blocked, but he hadn't disabled JavaScript, so I was able to trace him."

"Excellent!" I said.

Addison Clifton had been missing for over a week now, and I was excited that we might finally locate our HookedUp enigma. I glanced at my watch and saw it was only fifteen minutes until six.

"So who is he?" I asked.

I heard Kenz ruffle papers on his end. "Guy named Max Jondo. His address is 1906 Wright Street in Trouville."

My stomach dropped.

60

Detective Kennedy

What did I just hear?

"Shit," I whispered under my breath.

"Is there a problem?" Kenz asked.

"Yeah," I said. "But it's not yours. Good work, Kenz, and thanks, but I have to go."

I rang off and stood up, staring at the TV but no longer seeing it. How? Eddie and I'd been there, and I'd gone through every inch of that house, and there was no trace of a woman. Except….

I immediately called the crime lab and asked for Mulvaney, my usual go-to guy there, and also the one running the tests on the hair sample I'd found in Jondo's basement. I had to wait a bit before he came on the line.

"What's up, Ryan?" he asked.

"Please tell me you were able to ID that hair sample I sent," I said urgently.

"Yeah," he replied. "I sent you a report, and then I gave the info to Eddie over the phone. Didn't he tell you?"

"No, he didn't. When did you talk to him?"

"About twenty-five minutes ago. He said you'd already left for the day but that he'd pass it along," he said non-plussed.

What the fuck? Why didn't Eddie call me? But then Eddie was convinced Addison Clifton was already dead, so maybe he didn't feel it was urgent enough to contact me when I was off-duty. Still.

"What're the results?" I wanted to know.

"Human hair. Female."

"Did it match the missing person's hair samples I gave you?" I probed further.

"Perfect match."

Got the bastard.

"Thanks, Mulvaney, I appreciate it, but I gotta run," I said quickly and hung up.

Barbara Meade was right all along. I still couldn't quite believe it. However, she was the least of my concern right then.

I re-strapped my holster back on, grabbed my discarded jacket and headed for the door. I called Eddie but it went to his voice mail. I tried his private cell but got the same result. I'd keep trying him, but in the meantime I had to get to Jondo's.

61

Addison

The trees were just ahead of us.

"Come on, Cheryl, we're almost there!" I panted.

Suddenly another shot rang out behind us, and I felt something whizz beside my head. There was a sharp thwack in one of the trees ahead, causing shards of wood to explode outward.

Totally panicked, I risked a look over my shoulder and saw *him* and another man running after us. The second man had a gun in his hand. He raised his arm, preparing to fire at us again, and my heart thumped heavily against my chest. I turned away and ran faster.

Then something horrible happened.

Cheryl stopped running.

I felt and heard her do so before I looked back again. She faced the two men, her arms raised over her head in surrender.

"No!" I screamed, but I didn't stop. I put every ounce of strength I had left into my legs and pumped them even faster.

He ran faster, too. I could hear him gaining on me.

I made it through the first trees as another shot rang out behind me. My bare feet were cut into by the rocks and prickly undergrowth on the ground beneath me, but I didn't stop. However, I was forced to weave among the close ranks of trees, and that slowed me down. The trees, the very thing that promised to be a haven, seemed like they would end up being my downfall.

They were.

He was right behind me.

I heard a loud intake of breath, then suddenly he leapt onto me, throwing me to the ground. One side of my face was scraped by the rough bark of a tree as I hit the ground with a thud, pinned between the rocky ground and his heavy weight on top of me. The air was squeezed out of me momentarily, and I felt dazed and disoriented.

I heard a pitiful whining noise and realized it was coming from me. No, no, no! I'd been so close! I couldn't let him take me back again. I struggled and squirmed, trying to get out from beneath him, but he squeezed one of my wrists in a vice-like grip.

"You bitch!" he screamed.

He drove his other fist into one of my temples with the power of a runaway train.

Everything went black.

I was deep in a dark abyss, and as I was trying to climb out again I felt myself being dragged, first pavement and then grass, and finally the cool surface of cement. A small pinprick of light struggled to pierce the blackness enveloping me.

I could hear people talking above and around me, but they seemed so distant I couldn't make out what they were saying, it was just a hazy droning noise. Then the humming in my ears began to slowly dissipate and their words became clear.

"Is she breathing?" That was Cheryl.

"Yes, she's breathing." That was *him*. "Now shut up!"

My head was splitting, and for a moment I couldn't think why, then I remembered that bastard punching the side of my head. I also felt nauseous. I carefully peeled my eyes open but all I saw was a blurred sea of too bright light and moving shadows. I immediately closed them again and took a deep breath.

"I think she's coming around," said Cheryl.

"I told you to shut up," he snapped.

Someone bent over me and lightly slapped my cheek.

"Wake up," he said.

"You shouldn't have hit her so hard," said a male voice I didn't recognize. "Or you should've just killed her. Now we'll have to deal with her."

"She still has her uses," *Daddy* replied.

"Well, for Christ's sake, do something. We don't have a lot of time here, and a lot of shit to clean up," the other said gruffly.

I was slapped again, harder this time.

"Wake up, Addison."

I cracked my eyes open again and waited for my vision to clear. It took a moment. When it did I shut them quickly again. He was stooped over me, and the sight of his face made me want to throw up.

"Open your eyes, bitch!"

I felt him rise to his feet and I was kicked in the side, none too gently, so I finally forced my eyes to open.

I saw him, Cheryl and the man with the gun, which he still held, standing over me. Daddy looked furious, Cheryl looked scared and the unknown man was grim and serious. Seeing I was fully awake, Cheryl squatted down beside me.

"Why didn't you keep running?" I asked her weakly.

I really thought if I hadn't wasted time looking back after she stopped, I would have made it. She would have too if only she'd kept going and not surrendered.

Daddy bent down, his face twisted with animosity. "Cheryl knows the rules," he said.

"Come on, Max," said the other man. "You know what you've gotta do here, don't you?"

Max. So that was his name.

Max straightened up again. "Yes," he replied to the other in a detached voice.

"Also, you have to leave, man. And you can't ever come back here," the other continued.

"I know that," Max said between his teeth.

"And we have to get rid of the bodies," said the other.

The bodies? Did he mean me and Cheryl? My terror returned.

He moved from the circle over me and I watched as he pulled two shovels down from a hook on a wall. That's when I realized we must be in his garage. He crossed behind Cheryl and the strange man, opened one of his car's doors and stowed the shovels inside.

"What the fuck do you think I'm doing?" Max asked irritably. His head snapped in my direction. "Get up," he commanded me.

I slowly and painfully pushed myself up to a sitting position. I looked around me, and that's when I saw them.

Two dead bodies lying in a pool of blood! One of them was a cop. His head had been bashed in and was almost unrecognizable.

He must have been the one sent to answer my 911 call. I twisted around and immediately threw up. There wasn't much, I hadn't eaten in a while. I suddenly felt so guilty; I felt responsible for that policeman's death. My frantic call had brought him to this. My head was spinning, and my heart felt heavy.

I watched in mounting horror as Max bent down over one of the bodies, an old man, and lifted him in his arms, heedless of the blood that smeared his shirt and arms. He tossed him unceremoniously into the trunk of his car, then bent down and shoved his body as far back as it would go.

He then turned to the dead cop.

"Take off his belt," advised the other man.

Max nodded, bent down and removed the cop's belt, which held a gun in a holster. He tossed it to the other man, who deftly caught it in his free hand. He then got his hands around the cop's shoulders and tugged. He looked over at the other guy.

"You have to help, he's heavier, and I can't lift him alone," he said.

The other guy sighed, slung the cop's belt over his shoulder and thrust his own gun into a holster hidden under his jacket. He walked over and together the two men lifted the cop into the trunk. Max shoved him back against the other dead body. Both men were bloodied after handling them. The other guy looked at his blood smeared jacket in distaste, then at Max, who walked back in my direction and towered over me.

"Get in," he said without emotion.

I couldn't believe I'd heard him right. I looked toward the open trunk, completely panicked, then back up at him.

"W-what?" I stammered.

"Get in the trunk," he said tightly.

"Are you crazy?" I shouted and scooted backwards. "No!"

A tic pulled at one corner of his mouth. "They're dead. Yeah. Gross. I get it. Now, unless you want Buddy-boy to shoot you right now, get-the-fuck-in!"

The other man removed his gun again and trained it on me.

"You heard the man. Do it!" he ordered.

I got slowly to my feet, my whole body trembling violently. I looked over at Cheryl, but she stood very still, as if completely shocked at the turn of events. Her face was deathly pale.

"She can't help you," Max said.

I slowly walked toward the trunk on legs that felt like rubber. I stopped at the opening and looked at the two bodies inside. My insides twisted and I felt gooseflesh prick my arms and the back of my neck.

"For the last time — get in."

Stifling a keening whine, I crawled into the trunk and maneuvered so that my back was to the two dead men. It was a tight fit. Max walked over and looked down at me with no expression, then he slammed the hood down, leaving me in stifling darkness.

62

Addison

I lay there some time before I heard the engine start up and felt it being backed out of the garage. Soon the smooth asphalt was replaced with a bumpy, uneven surface. I was awfully conscious of the cold clammy flesh of the dead man behind me. It was spongy feeling, and I gagged several times. My panic was rising to a dizzying level. I could hardly breathe my chest was so tight, and I was becoming almost paralyzed with terror.

It felt like we drove on and on, and I lost all sense of time and space, just the knowledge of being enclosed with two dead men, like being entombed in a coffin. I could hear voices up front but couldn't make out the words over the hum of the engine and the small rocks being thrown by the wheels.

Finally, the car halted with a sharp jerk. I heard doors opening and almost immediately the hood of the trunk was thrown up. I blinked in the sudden light.

Max hovered over me. “Out,” he barked.

I couldn’t obey fast enough. I hurriedly scrambled out of the trunk. I saw one sleeve of my robe was covered in sticky blood and bile rose up my throat.

I looked around and saw we were in a small clearing in a wooded area, surrounded by nothing but a huge expanse of trees that seemed to march endlessly on in tall ranks, one after the other. There was another car parked next to the one I’d just escaped from.

The strange man and Cheryl were standing next to one another. Once again his gun was pointed at me. I wondered if this was finally it. My heart was thumping so violently I thought I might save them the effort and have a heart attack instead. I was so frightened I could barely keep myself standing upright, my legs felt like they might give out any minute.

“Cheryl!” Max yelled, and made a gesture for her to join him.

Cheryl started, looking nervous, then walked over to us in a slow, jerking gait.

“You two get those bodies out of there,” he ordered gruffly.

I shook my head and backed away. I’d already had as much contact as I wanted with the two dead men. Max reached out, grabbed my arm and shoved me roughly toward Cheryl.

The man called Buddy-boy came closer and cocked his gun. “I’d do what he says.”

Cheryl tugged at the sleeve of my robe that wasn’t soaked in blood.

Together we reached inside the trunk and pulled at the uniform of the dead cop. He was very heavy, and was wedged in so tight I wasn’t sure we’d ever manage to get him out. Cheryl had her arms under his shoulders while I tried to maneuver his legs out. We tugged and yanked until he came over the back of the trunk and fell to the ground with a dull thud.

I looked down at his lifeless mess of a face and wondered who he left behind. Who would mourn his passing? Parents or siblings? Was he married? Did he have children? I, of all people, knew what is was to lose people close to you. A lump formed in my throat.

"Good," said Max. "Now get the other one."

The other dead man was smaller and thinner, so we were able to get him out of the trunk with less effort than the cop. As he hit the ground and rolled to one side I wondered who he was. He looked old and frail.

Max reached into the backseat, pulled out the two shovels and immediately tossed one to Cheryl, who caught it awkwardly. He threw the remaining one at me. I didn't catch it, and was forced to lean over and retrieve it, hating to lose sight of Buddy-boy's gun as I did so. I expected to feel a bullet in my back any second.

"Start digging," Max ordered.

Cheryl slammed the shovel point first into the ground and gave him a defiant look, angry and disgusted.

"You do it," she retorted sharply. "I didn't kill anybody."

Buddy-boy took a step forward, aiming his revolver at her head.

I grabbed her arm and pulled her closer. "Cheryl," I warned softly.

The last thing I wanted was to watch her be killed before my eyes, though I knew we'd both be dead soon.

"Somebody better start digging a hole," said Buddy-boy between his teeth.

"Fuck you," she spit at him.

This was a side of her I hadn't seen before. I tightened my grip on her arm and leaned closer. "What's wrong with you?" I whispered urgently. "You want him to shoot you?"

Buddy-boy turned to Max and sighed in frustration. "I told you about her, didn't I? But you never fucking listen to me."

"Not now, Eddie," retorted Max, irritated.

I wanted to turn and flee, but I started to shake uncontrollably and my legs threatened to give out beneath me any second.

"Look at all the fucking trouble she's caused you," Buddy-boy continued. "None of this bullshit would've happened if you'd just listened to me. Now I can't help you anymore, you're in such deep shit. And all because of her!"

He gestured at me and Cheryl. Us? He kidnapped *us*, we didn't cause *any* of this!

"When have you ever helped?" growled Max.

"Oh, that's rich!" Buddy replied bitterly. "I covered for you the last three times you did this kind of shit. Hell, I even helped you bury that last girl. And don't forget I tipped you off that me and my partner were coming to your place a few days ago. How do you think that would've gone down if I hadn't? Kennedy would've found her and your ass would be in jail!" He stepped closer to Max and thrust his face at him. "*I* don't kill cops. I actually value my job, so I promise, I'd have cut you loose and let you swung. So don't fuck with me."

"He went into my house, not you. You could have insisted on being the one to go through the place. How was that *helping* me? What if he found something?"

Buddy-boy sneered. "He's the lead detective, so I couldn't exactly tell him what to do, but I knew you'd be thorough, and I gave you enough lead time to clean your shit up. I saved your ass that day. And how many other times have I covered for you, Max? Covered your sick little games. That shit's over. Now you're gonna have to run pretty damned far to keep your neck out of a noose, change your name, the whole shebang. *Get rid of her*. Now. She's really fucked you good this time."

"I'm going to. She's been nothing but trouble from the start," growled Max, and looked straight at me.

Buddy punched Max in the shoulder, knocking him back a little.

"You asshole. I'm not talking about her." He pointed to Cheryl. "I'm talking about *her*."

63

Barb

For the fourth time I looked up at my rearview mirror to make sure Luke was still following me. I was afraid that at any moment he would chicken out and double back, but so far he was keeping behind me.

One we got out of the city, it was a long drive to get to the house I believed was Addison's prison. We drove through a bunch of suburbs until we hit the countryside. It was pretty heavily wooded and felt desolate and lonely, with curving roads that had no other traffic and seemed to wind on and on in sinister solitude.

Finally I saw the steep hill I remembered from before and started up it, checking yet again that Luke was still there. My car crested the top and I saw the same house ahead and to my left. The garage door was open, but as I pulled my car to a stop beside the road in front of it I saw it was empty.

Shit.

It looked like he wasn't home.

But as Luke pulled up behind me and parked I decided that was a good thing. Maybe we could do some snooping during his absence and find Addison, or at least discover some evidence that she was being kept there.

I heard Luke's door opening and I got out of my own car and waited for him to join me. We stood staring at the house a moment, and my skin prickled. I'm sure it was partly my imagination, but I could almost feel ugly dark strands floating out from it to enfold me in their coils.

"Barb?" asked Luke.

I shook myself and glanced at him. He was giving me a funny look.

"What's wrong with you?" he continued.

"Nothing," I replied, and tried to give myself a mental slap.

He turned his attention to the house. "Looks like nobody's home." He gave me a sour look. "So we made this drive for nothing?"

"No, it's perfect," I replied.

"How do you figure?" he asked, giving me a sharp look.

"He's not here to stop us, so we're going to look inside!"

"Are you out of your mind?" he yelled.

I frantically waved at him to keep his voice down. "It's our opportunity, Luke, don't you see? If she's in there we can get to her while he's not around to stop us. We'll try all the doors, and even if they're locked you can jimmy one open. You told me you know how to do that sort of thing."

He took a very deep breath and dropped his head back, staring up at the sky. "That's breaking and entering, Barb. A misdemeanor at the very least."

"Luke —"

"No," he said firmly.

I stomped my foot in frustration. "Fine. If you're so worried about your precious job I'll do it by myself."

I headed up the path but he shot out his hand and grabbed my arm. "Sorry, Barb, can't let you do that."

"Oh, yeah?"

I spun around and gave him a hard swift kick in the shin. He yelped and released my arm. I made a dash for the garage. He was right behind me. But just inside I stopped so abruptly he ran into me, almost knocking me over. He opened his mouth to yell at me some more then saw what I was gaping at.

There was a huge pool of what could only be blood on the floor in front of us. It was also splattered about one wall and a shelf.

"Holy shit," he breathed softly.

64

Addison

Cheryl's face contorted into pure rage.

"You bastard!" she screamed at Buddy-boy and took a step back. She folded her arms and glared at him. "He doesn't run this show, asshole. *I do*."

What was she saying? I wasn't even sure I heard her correctly.

"Cheryl?"

"Shut up, you stupid slut," she hissed.

I stood there, paralyzed by shock. I felt like everything around me was spinning out of control.

"Cheryl, what're you saying?" I whispered through numb lips.

"What do you think, sweetheart?" she replied, smiling scornfully.

"I… I…."

She turned away from Buddy-boy to face me fully.

"We were looking for someone new. I wanted someone else, but he picked you. Want to know why?"

I backed away, resisting the urge to cover my ears. I didn't know what was going on, but it felt as though my long nightmare had gotten even darker and filthier. The look she was giving me was so full of hate it hit me like a blow in the face.

"It was your stupid safe word," she continued. "Mommy. He hated his mother — and for good reason. So he picked you to take the punishment." She leaned closer and her smile stretched wider. "But I told him what to do." She laughed at me derisively, then looked over her shoulder at Buddy-boy. "Some people need reminding that I've always been in charge here."

The kidnapping. The confinement. The repeated rapes. The dog cage. The beating. The honey. She made those things happen?

It was all Cheryl.

I couldn't believe what I was hearing, couldn't take it in, as though someone had just told me the dirt beneath my feet was actually water.

"Why?" I rasped hoarsely.

She laughed. "It's a game, Addison. He likes to fuck. I like to watch and manipulate. It's like chess, and every move has consequences, only I'm the one moving the pieces and you're the one losing. Of course, you know all about poor moves, don't you, Addison?" She laughed scornfully. "You signed on to that site, even though you knew it was dangerous. So if you think about it, all of this is really your own fault. You thought everything was safe, but you didn't know about me. I was there in the shadows, making all the moves, deciding your fate. And I have to say, this particular game was fun. Until it wasn't anymore."

"And look where she's gotten you with her stupid games!" Buddy-boy spat at Max in angry frustration. "Get. Rid. Of. Her." Then he fixed his eye on Cheryl. "Start digging, bitch. And make sure it's a really big hole." He cocked his revolver. "Big enough for *four*."

"Buddy —" began Max uncomfortably.

"Shut up, Max. Someone has to take control of this situation," Buddy-boy snapped at him. He took a menacing step toward Cheryl. "Dig."

Cheryl stared at him then turned to Max for support. "Max?" she asked querulously.

He gave her a mournful look, then he turned away.

"Max!" she screamed, then let her mouth fall open in shock, realizing the betrayal.

Buddy-boy stepped over to her. "You're done with all that shit. Now pick up that fucking shovel."

Cheryl began to cry.

"Do it!"

She reached down and retrieved the shovel with a badly shaking hand.

I wanted to feel sorry for her, but all I felt was revulsion and fury. I still couldn't believe her duplicity.

All that time together, and she had been secretly enjoying it, enjoying my suffering and pain. What kind of person did that? Someone without a soul.

I watched her dispassionately as she fumbled with the shovel, her fear making her clumsy and moving like she was drunk.

Buddy-boy stepped forward and kicked at the cop's corpse. "Get these in the ground." Then he suddenly stopped and stared down at the body on the ground.

His gaze was so full of surprise everyone craned to see what he was looking at.

Everyone but me.

"What — is — that?" he demanded, a stunned note in his voice.

65

Detective Kennedy

As I crested the hill I saw two cars parked on the side of the road in front of the house and slowed, wondering what was going on. Erring on the side of caution I pulled off a good distance from them. It was always smart to expect the worst, especially now that I knew Jondo was a kidnapper and who knew what else.

I got out of my car, careful to close the door as quietly as possible so as not to alert anyone of my presence. I unsnapped my holster and brought out my revolver, checking to make sure the safety was off, then strode quickly forward.

As I neared I heard voices drifting out of the open garage and brought my gun to the ready. I hastened my steps and drew near the opening, flattening my back against the wall adjacent to the open area.

"What the fuck, Luke?" asked a woman in a nervous voice.

I sighed and hung my head.

It was Barbara Meade.

"Get in your car and go home," replied a male voice I wasn't familiar with. "I have to call this in."

I moved behind the two people standing just inside the garage.

"Don't move," I ordered in a commanding voice.

"Shit!" That was Meade, who whipped her head around to look at me.

"Hands up where I can see them," I continued.

The man standing next to her, whose back was to me complied immediately, but Barbara swung around and frowned.

"What're you doing here?" she wanted to know.

"I'd like to ask you the same," I replied.

"Well—" she began but the man next to her cut her off.

"Permission to turn around?" he called back to me.

"Slowly," I responded, "And keep your hands where I can see them."

"Yes, sir."

The man turned and faced me. He looked to be in his mid to late thirties, clean cut and well built.

"My name's Luke Miller," the man said. "I'm a cop." Then his face changed as recognition set in. "You're Detective Ryan Kennedy."

"Don't know you," I said. Always verify. "What unit?"

"Patrol division," he answered quickly.

"Whose your CO?" I probed further, knowing anyone could claim to be a policeman.

"Dwayne Orloff," he snapped back quickly.

I lowered my gun and gave him a hard look. "What're you doing here, officer?" I asked.

"She—"

"I made him come," she said swiftly. "It's not his fault."

"Sir," said Luke quickly. "There's something you need to see."

He stepped aside and I got a good look into the empty garage.

Shit.

66

Addison

Max edged over to Buddy-boy, whose attention was fixed on the dead cop's right leg, specifically his ankle. Strapped around it was a small holster, but what caused him concern was the fact that it was *empty*.

There was a loud retort of a gun being fired.

Cheryl cried out and clutched her diaphragm. Blood seeped through her fingers as she looked over at me, completely shocked. I watched impassively as she slowly crumpled to the ground.

The two men whipped their heads around as one, first to Cheryl on the ground, then over to me.

I was holding the missing gun in my hands, and it was now aimed at them.

I saw the small weapon when Cheryl and I removed the dead cop's body from the trunk. I swiftly unsnapped the strap securing it and slipped it into the pocket of my robe. Cheryl never even noticed.

Without a word I trained it on Buddy-Boy and fired. His eyes went wide and then he fell onto the ground. It wasn't a perfect aim, I had been going for his head, but it hit him on one side of his chest. I knew that because I saw the blood spurt out. It gave me immense satisfaction. But not as much as what I intended to do next.

Max looked stunned.

I turned the weapon on him and fired.

I was too late.

Just as I was pulling the trigger Max dived toward his fallen half-brother and groped under his body. I quickly realized he was trying to get to his half-brother's gun, which was under him. I couldn't let that happen.

I shot again, and this time the bullet hit flesh. I'd hit him in his right arm, causing him to jerk back from his brother.

I was shaking all over, half from fear and half from vengeful exhilaration, but I took a step closer and aimed again. I wasn't going to miss this time.

Max scrambled to his feet, clutching his wounded arm. "Come on, Addison, be a good girl and —"

"Fuck you, asshole!" I said and pulled the trigger.

Shit! I missed him completely.

Siezing his opportunity he darted away, running toward the thick woods edging the clearing.

I looked after him, then at Cheryl and Buddy-boy's still bodies. I stepped over to them and looked down at Cheryl. I couldn't tell if she was still breathing or dead, and at that moment I really didn't care.

"Like you said before," I said to her, "Some people are just sick fucks." Then I spit on her. She deserved worse.

I glanced back up and saw Max hobbling painfully as he neared the tree line. Suddenly I was filled with a hot, searing rage so fierce I thought I would explode, and began to run after him.

Though feeling drunk with my desire for revenge, my brain ran through the number of shots I'd fired. I counted five. I had no idea how many rounds the small gun I carried held. I decided it didn't matter. If they were all gone, I'd kill him with a rock or my bare hands if I had to.

I was still ten yards away when he disappeared into the trees.

I cursed, urging myself to run faster, and soon I encountered the first tree. Hundreds of little needles whipped across my cheek as I passed it, and the scent of pine resin was strong. The woods were dense, a mixture of pines, maples and other kinds I didn't know, and I was forced to wind around one every few feet. I could still see him ahead, but knew I was too far away to try and shoot.

Drops and splashes of blood on the ground and the leaves left me a trail whenever he disappeared from sight. He was running for his life, but I could hear the whisper of his ragged breath, and knew he would inevitably be forced to slow down.

Suddenly I couldn't see him anymore.

There was no way I was going to let that bastard get away.

I ran even faster but kept a keen eye on the trail of blood. After several minutes I realized I wasn't seeing his blood anymore and stopped. I was breathing heavily as I looked all around, trying to see where he went to.

Suddenly there was a loud crash to my left and he exploded out of a huge cluster of bushes and tackled me to the ground.

Summoning every ounce of strength I had, I wrestled furiously with him. Despite his weakness, he was overpowering me and finally managed to wrest the gun from me. I groped wildly and frantically with my free hand until it finally closed over a good sized rock. I scooped it up and hammered the side of his face with it. He jerked back and the gun slid from his grasp.

I became like a feral animal, and quick as lightening grabbed back the gun. I scrambled to my feet and pointed it at him.

Max raised an arm in supplication. "Please…," he panted in a weakened voice.

I fired.

His crotch exploded with blood and gore, and he shrieked with intense agony.

I fired again. But this time nothing happened.

The gun was empty.

Feeling detached, I casually tossed the gun aside, bent down and retrieved my discarded rock, dropping to my knees beside him. I raised it and brought it down on his head as hard as I could. It did it over and over and over again.

I finally got to my feet and looked down at the mangled mess that had been his face, then turned and silently limped away.

I felt unreal, as if walking through a thick fog until I saw the clearing ahead. I didn't even know how I'd made it back there, I had been on auto pilot. I stumbled out of the trees and continued to limp my way toward the two cars.

My breathing changed, becoming shallow and quick. My whole body began to tremble uncontrollably, suddenly feeling chilled to the bone.

Then it hit me.

I was finally free!

I came to an abrupt awkward stop. A hurricane of wild emotions roared through me, paralyzing me momentarily.

I was free.

But I had also killed three people.

I dropped to my knees and tears flooded down my cheeks. I leaned back on my heels, let my head drop back and looked up at the twilit sky.

67

Barb

Luke was awkwardly patting my back, trying to get me to calm down. He wasn't doing a very good job of it.

When Luke showed Kennedy the blood splattered around the garage it hit me suddenly that it must have belonged to Addison. That man had killed her!

I dissolved into a slobbering hysterical mess.

I hated breaking down like this in front of him and that detective, but I couldn't help it. Addy was gone, all that blood had to be proof of it. We'd been such close friends for most of my life, I wasn't sure I could handle losing her. It almost felt like half of me had been brutally severed.

Kennedy took pictures with his phone then called the police station. I didn't bother to listen to his words I was so upset. Then he backed us away from the garage and walked around the side of the house. He came back a few minutes later looking very grave.

Luke gave him a questioning look.

"A patrol unit was sent here in response to a 911 call," he said in answer to Luke's look. He gestured over his shoulder. "His patrol car is parked behind the house."

They both stared at the blood again.

What was he inferring? That the blood in there might belong to a police officer? A chill went through me, followed by something like hope. Did that mean that Addy….

Suddenly there was a loud report off in the distance. It sounded like a gun shot.

Detective Kennedy spun around and gazed toward the trees across the street. That's where it sounded like the noise had come from. He was tense, and I noticed Luke drew himself to stiff attention as well.

"What was—?" I began.

I was interrupted by another gun shot, followed a moment later by another one.

What the hell was going on?

"Stay here!" snapped Kennedy, looking directly back at me. Then he looked over at Luke. "You have a sidearm in your car?" he asked him.

"Yes, sir," answered Luke promptly. "Never go anywhere without it."

He took off at a run, followed by Kennedy, who waited while Luke opened his door and came back out with a holster and revolver that he quickly strapped on.

"Let's go," commanded Kennedy and they both took off running toward the woods.

"Hey!" I yelled at the two of them.

"Stay there, Ms. Meade!" Kennedy yelled back. "I'm not fooling around!"

"He means it, Barb!" added Luke over his shoulder.

The two of them ran so fast they crossed the street and hit the trees in record time.

I stood there staring after them, frowning. I looked back at the gore filled garage behind me and felt a shiver crawl up and down my spine, and something occurred to me. What if the owner of the house came back?

Fuck that.

I took off after the two men, running as fast as I could, which wasn't that fast unfortunately; I enjoyed way too many hot dogs and fast food. I made a mental note to start eating healthier.

I hit the trees and stopped a moment, trying to catch my breath. I scanned the thick trees, trying to discover where they'd gone, but they were already out of sight. I didn't think I'd find them in all that.

Well, shit.

I couldn't go after them, but I sure as shit wasn't going back to that house. No way.

I hugged my arms tightly, looking all around and jerking at every unexpected sound. I hoped they'd be back soon.

68

Detective Kennedy

Officer Miller and I were darting through trees, rushing toward the direction of the gunshots. I glanced over at the man once, and I was reassured by his calm but purposeful demeanor; he was obviously a well-trained police officer. We ran for quite a long time. I was concerned at the absolute quiet that followed those gunshots, that wasn't a good sign. I hoped we weren't about to stumble upon a bad scene, but was fairly certain that would be the case.

To his credit, Officer Miller didn't try to make any conversation, just kept his gun at the ready and remained alert for any sign of danger. We kept a steady jog in silence.

Finally we broke the trees and found ourselves in a small clearing surrounded on all sides with thick woods. In the middle of the clearing were two vehicles. I recognized one of them as belonging to

Max Jondo; I'd seen it on my last visit to his house. The other one seemed familiar somehow, but at the moment I couldn't place it.

We slowed our pace and walked steadily forward. Suddenly, Officer Miller tapped my arm and nodded his head toward the parked vehicles. I immediately saw what he had seen. A foot laying upon the ground extended beyond one of the Volvo's back wheels.

We cautiously made our way forward and edged past the car.

"Christ," I muttered.

There were three dead bodies scattered on the ground, one of which was a woman wearing a bathrobe; she had been shot in the stomach. I had no idea who she was, she wasn't Addison Clifton. She didn't match her pictures at all.

Officer Miller immediately got to his knees beside her and checked her vital signs. He looked up and shook his head.

"Shit," I swore.

He quickly shifted to the man in a patrol officer's uniform and did the same thing. His face hardened.

"He's gone," he said tersely.

He didn't even have to check the other man, he was plainly dead.

Miller stood up and gazed at the carnage. "What the hell happened here?"

"I don't know," I replied heavily. "I guess we'll find out in time."

Miller gazed out at the clearing and suddenly stiffened. "Detective Kennedy," he said and motioned with his chin toward the far side of the clearing.

I followed his gaze and saw her.

A woman, also wearing a bathrobe, was sitting in a child's pose, her knees beneath her, her head on the ground and arms wrapped around her chest, as though in some protective cocoon.

"Stay here," I commanded him and ran toward her.

She lifted her head as I neared. Her face was badly bruised, and one side of her lower lip was swollen. Her eyes were puffy from crying. I gently lowered myself beside her.

"Addison?" I queried softly.
She gave me a dazed look, then finally nodded slowly.
Thank God!

69

Addison

"I want to go home," I said crossly.

The nurse standing next to my bed fiddling with my IV tube glanced at me. "The doctor's making his rounds and should be here shortly," she replied in a neutral tone. "You can take it up with him."

When the detective and that other policeman found me in the clearing I was numb with shock. They drew me away from the carnage, and Kennedy draped my shoulders with his jacket.

"Can you walk?" he asked.

I nodded.

The man with him stayed at the scene with the dead bodies, and Kennedy carefully guided me back the long way through the woods and across the street.

Someone barreled into me and I was swept into a passionate bearhug, hurting my wounded back and causing me to wince. It took me a moment to realize it was Barb. I hugged her back fiercely and we both dissolved into hot tears that blended together as our faces pressed each other. I never wanted to let her go.

She pulled back and saw my bruised face and the black eye Daddy had given me earlier; I guessed from her expression of horror that I must have looked awful.

"Oh, Addy," she whispered tearfully. "What did that bastard do to you?"

We continued forward, Barb clutching one arm, and Kennedy on my other side, but at the sight of that dreadful house I balked. Kennedy spoke in soft words and gently guided me toward a car parked far away on the side of the road. Just as he opened the door I heard a loud screech and flinched violently, jerking around, expecting some new menace.

Several vehicles with sirens fixed to their roofs topped the hill. They all quickly parked along the road. They turned out to be crime scene investigators. Kennedy passed me off to a middle aged woman, who immediately drove me to the hospital.

A doctor examined me and I fell into an exhausted sleep. I don't know how long I slept but when I woke Detective Kennedy was sitting beside my bed.

He asked me to tell my story and I did, telling it over and over again until he finally seemed satisfied and left.

I was in the first of the two beds in the room, so I immediately saw Detective Kennedy when he walked in the next day. After another glance at me the nurse left the room. He came to my side and looked down.

"How're you feeling this morning?" he asked.

I frowned and didn't answer.

He nodded, as if he understood my mood. "I'm sorry, Ms. Clifton. I know you've had quite a terrible experience. I really wish we could've found you sooner."

"That makes two of us," I replied sourly.

He simply nodded again. “The doctor said they’d be sending for a mental health specialist.”

“No!” I said sharper than I meant to. Cheryl had claimed to be one, and the thought made me want to retch.

“Well… I guess that’s up to the doctor.”

“No,” I repeated firmly. “No therapists.”

He started to say something then thought better of it. He motioned to a nearby chair. “Mind if I sit?”

I nodded okay and he pulled the chair over to the bed and sat down.

“I know this was very traumatic, and I appreciate you going through your story so many times. I understand that’s hard.”

He had no idea.

I looked at him and part of me wanted to lash out. At that moment, men, any man, made me so angry. Then I took a deep breath and tried to relax. It wasn’t his fault, and I really did know that all men weren’t like Max Jondo. Besides, Kennedy was just trying to do his job.

“Did you find anything in… that house? The things I told you about?” I asked.

“Yes,” he replied. “We also retrieved a lot of evidence on his computer. Unfortunately, you weren’t the first woman he held in captivity.”

“I figured.”

“Why is that?”

“Just some of the things he said,” I replied. “Or Cheryl did.”

All kinds of horrible images reared in my mind. Dozens of women’s faces, screaming and begging for mercy. And all the while Cheryl sitting like a spider, hiding her smiles.

“How…?” I began, then swallowed. I was going to ask him how many women before me, but I decided I didn’t want to know.

He seemed to sense what was going through my mind. “You were lucky, Ms. Clifton.”

I didn't feel lucky. I knew what he meant though. He meant those women were dead.

"There is one thing that's not adding up…," he began, then paused.

I looked at him nervously, wondering if he was getting ready to accuse me of murder. That had worried me all morning. After all, I did kill Cheryl and Buddy-boy in cold blood. The fact that they had planned to kill me first didn't mean I wasn't guilty.

"Am I…," I swallowed hard. "Am I in trouble?" I asked anxiously.

He looked surprised.

"Are you going to charge me for murder?"

That seemed to surprise him. "No, it was self-defense."

The relief was immediate and I sighed.

I hadn't told the police the entire truth. I didn't tell them that I had chased Max down, that he had run from me and my lust for revenge. I didn't tell them I enjoyed killing him.

"No," he continued, "It's the clearing in the woods. We swept the entire area and—"

"You *did* find Max Jondo, didn't you?" I asked, sitting up in alarm, my voice almost pleading.

"Yes, ma'am. We also tagged the woman, the man and the dead cop. That was three near the cars. Are you certain there was four of them?"

I wasn't sure what he meant. I wrinkled my forehead. "There was Cheryl and his half-brother, who he called Buddy-boy, and then the two men he killed in his garage, the policeman and the other guy."

"Well, we only found three, including the police officer. We didn't find the other guy. Do you know who he was, and could he have still been alive?"

I shook my head. "No, I never saw him before yesterday. But I was pretty sure he was dead. He certainly looked like it. Cheryl and I were forced to pull him out of the trunk and…,"

I stopped, once again feeling the cold, clammy skin and the unyielding weight of him and the cop. Their skin was a strange waxy white, and there was a sticky sweet odor about them and the all-pervasive iron smell of the congealing blood. The old man's arms were bent at an awkward angle, as though he were a puppet that had been dropped. I shuddered.

"I promise, he really looked dead," I finally said. "Could someone else have taken the body?" Then I shook my head. Who? The idea was silly. "I was so upset, maybe he just looked dead and came to, saw the others and left. I don't know. None of it makes sense."

"That's what we need to find out," he replied and stood up. "I'll let you get some more rest, but I'm sorry to say you'll be required to testify at the inquest."

"Okay," I replied listlessly.

"But don't worry," he went on. "It'll be several days from now. It will also be private. No jury or reporters, just the judge, me, a few police officers and you."

"Fine."

I was suddenly very tired. After falling into that first deep sleep I'd woken suddenly and couldn't return to it. I was terrified that at any moment I'd wake up and my rescue would all be a dream, that I was still a prisoner in that house, and so I was afraid to close my eyes.

However the sleep deprivation was beginning to take its toll on me and as soon as Detective Kennedy left my eyes began to feel heavy and were soon drooping. I was finally pulled under into the blessed forgetfulness of slumber.

"Hey, girl!"

My eyes popped open to see Barb standing by my bed. She was grinning ridiculously from ear to ear, and she ran a hand softly down one of my arms.

"Hi," I said weakly, wondering what time it was.

I glanced at the blinds and it looked like late afternoon.

Her grin disappeared and was swiftly replaced by worry. "Are you… um, how're you doing?" she asked tentatively.

"Barb?"

"Yeah?"

"Get me out of here. I want to go home."

"I'm on it."

She disappeared as quickly as she had appeared, and I sighed contentedly. I was certain Barb wouldn't let anybody, not the police or even that damn doctor bully her.

70

Addison

I was right.

An hour later I was sitting in the passenger side of her car, being driven home.

Home.

I'd been kept in captivity only for a little over a week — at least I thought so, but time felt so distorted. I felt like I'd been trapped in that house of horrors for years. I wondered if my own house would still feel like home to me, or if everything had changed. Then I decided that no, the house would be the same — it was me who had changed. Irrevocably.

I knew I'd never be the woman I once was, not the happy one with a husband and son, and not even the sad one who emerged after they left.

I was now a wounded woman with scars beyond those of my back.

I just hoped I could still face living. I'd seen those people before, the ones walking around but not really there, the ones who'd been hurt so badly they existed in sheltered limbo to hide from the pain, afraid to make eye contact, afraid to smile or feel anything at all lest the monsters overtake them.

I was also afraid I'd be trapped into a constant state of paranoia, afraid of every shadow, every noise, every man who looked my way.

"I'm so glad you're finally safe," Barb said abruptly. "All I've been doing the whole time you were… gone, is pray. And you know I'm not the religious type. Not sure if I even believe in God, but I didn't want to take any chances, you know?"

I smiled. "Thanks, Barb."

She snorted. "Made a whole lotta promises if He brought you back."

"I appreciate it," I said quietly, and realized for the first time what she herself must have gone through. If things had been reversed I would have been worried sick.

"I gotta quit drinking now, and I think I might be a vegetarian. I've got the list at home. I just hope I can still swear."

I laughed a little, and realized with a pang it was the first time in a very long time that I'd laughed. That hurt.

"I was so worried," she continued. "If you can believe it I lost seven pounds because I was so worried I couldn't eat. Well, mostly. I think there was a hot dog or two somewhere in there. And maybe some beer."

I placed a gentle hand on her arm. "I know. I'm sorry."

"Fuck that! It wasn't your fault, it was that prick who took you!"

I turned away and looked out the window at the passing houses. "I know," I said.

"I hope you pissed on his dead body!"

I said nothing, trying to block out the image of Max's mangled, pulpy face.

"Addy?"

"Yeah?" From her tone I had a feeling I knew what she was about to say, and I also knew she felt hesitant about saying it.

"Please promise you'll be more careful from now on. Don't go back to… you know."

The very idea made my skin crawl.

"Never," I said sharply.

"Good," she responded with a sigh of relief. She was silent a moment then said, "The accident, Matt and Justin… I know you thought you lost everything then, but…. You still have people who love you." I felt her look over at me. "You matter a lot to them."

I finally returned her look and tried to smile. "You mean you, Barb."

She nodded and returned her eyes to the road. "You just… gotta find your way back. Even if you have to fight for it. You know?"

I squeezed her arm. "I love you, too."

I was almost afraid to walk in through my own front door. Barb saw my hesitation so she took it upon herself to unlock it and throw it open.

"The police found your car. They went through everything and then I was able to get it, your car, I mean. It's in your garage. I got your purse, too."

She looked at me and I said, "Thanks."

"They found it in the dumpster of that motel. Did Kennedy tell you they saw them on the motel lobby camera? That asshole and his sick girlfriend? Looks like they scoped out the place before he met with you. I wish she wasn't dead because I'd like to kill her myself."

I said nothing.

"Also, Sarah said your job's waiting for you whenever you want it, but to take all the time you need."

She was talking frantically, like she was afraid to let silence take over.

I stepped inside and looked around. Everything was exactly like I'd left it, but it felt strange, alien almost. I ran a finger across a small table in the entry way. I looked back at her.

"You cleaned." She nodded. "You don't clean your own place, Barb."

"I thought it was the least I could do," she mumbled.

I finally turned and hugged her tightly. "I know everything you did, Kennedy told me," I said, my face buried in her neck. "He said he's never known such a pest. He also said you went there, knowing you were putting yourself in danger. Thank you, Barb."

She hugged me back then shook her head. "I felt like I wasn't doing enough." She suddenly looked uncomfortable. "What do you say, Addy? Want a drink?"

I smiled. "I thought you gave that up," I replied.

She shrugged. "Well, God knows I'm not the type to be trusted with promises."

She marched into the kitchen. I remained where I was, looking around the living room. For the first time I realized how bare and stark it was. No pictures or paintings on the wall, all the furniture and even the large area rug in shades of gray. It looked depressing. Worse, it mirrored the way I felt inside.

Barb returned with two tumblers of brandy. She handed me one, clinked it with her own glass and took a large swallow. I took a sip, relishing the burn at the back of my throat.

"I put on some water for tea—"

"No tea!" I retorted sharply.

She was taken aback and I fought to quell my rising panic. I knocked back my drink and handed her the empty glass. "I think I'll take a shower."

"Sure," she said, looking uncertain.

I was halfway to the bathroom when I turned back. "Barb? Would you… would you stay with me tonight."

"It was my plan all along. Already packed my toothbrush."

I felt immensely relieved. “Thank you.”

I stood under water so hot it was almost unbearable. I’d already had a shower at the hospital, but I felt like I would never be clean again. I frantically scrubbed every inch of my body. I stayed in the shower until the water began to get cold.

I grabbed a towel and stepped out, wrapping myself firmly in it. I was wiping the fog from the mirror when I saw a robe hung on the back of the bathroom door. I stared at it for a long, long moment, then walked over and yanked it from its hook. I wadded it in a ball, stuffed it into the waste basket and hurriedly left the room.

71

Addison

I stepped inside the bedroom and was relieved to see Barb had closed all the blinds. I had a feeling in the coming days and nights I'd be hiding from the world. Maybe in time I would see the mental health specialist everyone thought I should, but I wasn't ready yet.

I dropped the towel and slipped on a pair of panties. Being able to put them on gave me a feeling of security I hadn't had in what felt like months.

The door opened behind me.

"Holy shit!" cried Barb.

I looked over my shoulder at her, my forehead creased. "What's wrong?"

She moved toward me and very softly ran her finger down my scarred back.

"God, Addy. What did that monster do to you?"

I walked away, opened another drawer and quickly pulled on a tee-shirt, followed by a pair of sweatpants.

"I can't talk about it," I replied quietly.

"Sure, honey," she said softly, "I understand."

I turned and looked at her.

"No, you don't. Nobody does."

Not knowing how to respond, she just nodded and quietly left the bedroom.

I moved to the bedside table and slowly opened the drawer. I looked inside and stayed like that for I don't know how long. Then I reached in and removed the photo of my dead husband and son. I stared at Matt and Justin's smiling faces, touching Matt's lips, then set it on top of the table, where I'd be sure to see it every night.

I was never going to hide it again.

I found Barb in the kitchen looking inside the fridge. "I went to the store but didn't get a whole lot. I thought I'd wait until you could tell me what you wanted. So it looks like we're having bacon and eggs for supper."

I shrugged. "I'm not that hungry."

She looked pointedly at my body. I knew I'd visibly lost weight.

"You're gonna eat anyway," she commanded.

I smiled. "Okay."

There was a soft sound from somewhere else in the house. I jerked nervously. "What was that?" I asked in a hoarse voice.

She raised an eyebrow. "What?"

"I thought I just heard something, like a door opening."

"I didn't hear anything," she replied, then seemed to notice my agitation. "It was probably just the house settling, but I'll go check."

She left the room, but not without a worried backward glance at me.

I stood in the empty kitchen not knowing what to do. It felt like I was out of practice with normal living. So I opened the cabinet that held the alcohol. I spied the whiskey, but it reminded me of those nights in the motel with Max, and I shuddered. I didn't think I'd ever drink it again. Instead I took down the bottle of brandy and poured another shot. But before I could drink it Barb returned.

"Take it easy," she said when she saw the alcohol. "There's no one here. Like I said, just house noises."

My palms felt sweaty but I nodded okay.

Barb pointed at the back door. "Okay, I'm gonna go out back and grab a smoke then I'll make us supper. Holler if you want me." She moved to the door then looked back at me. "You gonna be okay?"

I nodded. "Yeah."

As soon as the door closed I drained the brandy and stared dully at the empty glass for a moment. The silence, broken only by the low droning hum of the refrigerator, felt oppressive. I stood there feeling lost and alien in my own home. Then slowly I became aware of a new noise. Faint squeaks on the wood floor of the living room. It was soft footsteps.

I panicked, starting for the back door when I stopped myself. I realized I was imagining things that weren't there, and I couldn't allow myself to be overcome with paranoia. Barb had just been in there and said the house was empty. I took a deep breath and forced myself to calm down.

My house was a 1920's craftsman, and it had always had odd sounds, especially at night or when the house settled due to temperature changes. I'd gotten so used to them over the years that I barely heard them anymore, but I didn't recognize them now. It really did sound like footsteps in the other room. It was irrational, but I felt the hair on my neck rise and goosebumps on my arms. I had to check for myself.

I moved slowly toward the arch that led to the living room and paused just inside the kitchen, straining my ears to listen.

Then I heard it again. Only this time it was the definite squeak of a shoe.

I felt my survival instincts kick in, and kick *hard*. I began backing away, carefully scanning the darkened room beyond, wishing desperately I'd turned every lamp in the place on.

I heard the faint rustle of clothing. A voice in my brain began screaming.

I suddenly whirled and dashed further back into the kitchen. I turned to the back door, meaning to escape that way, when I glanced at the toaster sitting on the counter. It was polished chrome, and at that moment worked just like a mirror.

I heard nothing but saw him reflected in it, coming straight at me!

He was pulling out his gun.

I scrambled for my set of knives in their holder on the counter, and I grabbed the largest one. Whirling around I faced him.

Buddy-Boy.

Alive, not dead as I'd believed.

"You killed my brother, bitch. Nobody fucks with my family."

His finger moved to the trigger as I lunged at him.

72

Barb

I was in the back yard when I heard a ferocious howl and the sound of a gunshot.

"Oh, my god!" I screamed, tossing away the joint I was smoking and rushed back towards the house.

I dashed inside and was stopped, paralyzed at the sight that met my eyes. I blinked rapidly. Fucking god!

A man was lying face down on the kitchen floor. Blood was spilling from beneath his body, trickling its way toward my feet.

"Addison!" I screamed as I fumbled in my pocket for my phone. I dialed 911 with badly shaking fingers. "Addison!" I screamed again.

She didn't answer.

"911," answered an operator. "What's your emergency?"

"Addison!" I called again and began to gingerly step around the body on the floor.

"Hello?" urged the operator. "Hello? Talk to me, please."

I stepped into some of the blood and immediately gagged.

"Ma'am!" said the operator.

I took a deep breath and forced myself to answer her. "There's been a… somebody's… here…," I babbled incoherently.

"Is there an intruder in your place?" she asked.

"Y-y-yes," I answered.

I was feeling dizzy. I hastily stepped out of my boots, not wanting to be anywhere near the growing pool of blood, and hopped all the way around him and out of the kitchen.

Then I saw her.

Addison was standing a few feet away, her tee-shirt and sweatpants covered in blood.

I dropped the phone and rushed over to her, grabbing her shoulders.

"Oh, my god. Are you hurt?"

She didn't answer, just stared dully at me.

From the floor the operator's voice drifted over to us. "Ma'am, you need to tell me, is the intruder still there?"

Addison, still gripping the bloody knife, stood there almost catatonically, then began to walk back into the kitchen, her movements jerky like a zombie. I retrieved my fallen phone and followed, my legs feeling all shaky.

Addison was looking down at the dead man. There was no expression on her face. It was as if she had left her body, looking but seeing nothing.

"What happened?" I asked unsteadily.

Addison slid down one of the cabinets to the floor, one of her feet resting in the widening pool of blood.

Addison stared in front of her at nothing at all.

"Ma'am!" I could hear the operator persisting. "Answer me, please. Is the intruder still there?"

I looked at the man lying on the floor, the blood pooling all around him.

"Yes," I continued, a catch in my voice. "He's still here."

73

Addison

Four months had gone by since I killed Detective Lemuche, aka Buddy-boy.

The police came and did what they do. Detective Kennedy was called once the body had been identified, and when he saw his former partner lying on my kitchen floor he visibly paled. He looked even worse after hearing my story.

In the hospital we had been at cross purposes. When he told me one of the bodies in the woods had gone missing, I thought it was the old man he was talking about, not Buddy-boy. Of course, he didn't know the survivor that slipped away was his partner, and neither did I. He was so dumbfounded he almost seemed in a daze. I would've felt sorry for him if I'd had any feeling left.

I didn't see Kennedy again until the inquest, where I was absolved of any wrong doing. It was pronounced self-defense, which in Lemuche's case it was. Since I didn't go into the details of Max's death, pleading fear, shock and memory loss, the verdict there was the same. I think Kennedy guessed at the savage glee of my revenge against Max; honestly, anyone looking at the pulp that was his face would, but he said nothing.

Barb hovered around me like a mother hen, refusing to leave my side until I reminded her that her mortgage wasn't going to pay itself. She went back to work but called me several times each day to make sure I was okay.

I didn't go back to Jergins & Co. I had a small savings and Matt's life insurance to fall back on for a while. And anyway, I had no desire to pick up my old life.

Cheryl told me trauma could cause avoidance from people, but that's not what this was. At least I didn't think so. I decided it was time to move on. Cheryl also said that the only way I could gain control of my life again was by surviving, that I owed it to Matt and Justin.

She might have been the world's worst bitch, but she was right about that.

It was time I started living again.

Letter to Readers

I'd like to thank you for choosing to read *Addison Chained.* I hope you loved it, and if you did I'd greatly appreciate a review. I would love to hear your thoughts on it, and it gives new readers a better insight into what they're getting themselves into.

You can follow me and keep in touch at:

Victorialhicksauthor.com

Facebook.com/victoria.l.hicks.writer

Instagram.com/victoria.l.hicks.author

Goodreads/Victoria_L_Hicks

Thanks!
Victoria

ACKNOWLEDGEMENTS

First, I have to thank my husband, Kevin, who suffers through my first drafts, and who also creates such kick-ass covers for me. Love you, honey! To my daughter, who promises to read my books (and doesn't), but always cheers me on with enthusiasm. To my son, who is actually attempting to read my first book, *String Dolls*, and says it vaguely reminds him of Goosebumps (bless his heart). Honestly, it's not for young adults.

A big shout-out and heartfelt thanks to my Beta readers, SueLin Kalisch, Rachel Browning and Vanessa Keck — you ladies rock! You were so insightful and detail oriented, and you helped more than you know.

Last but not least, to everyone who has ever read one of my books, including this one. Thank you.

About the Author

Victoria L Hicks is a voracious reader, and has been since she learned to read. Born in Hawaii and raised in Texas, she lived in New York City, Los Angeles, and a teeny little town in Colorado that if you blinked you'd miss it, before settling in the Finger Lakes region of New York with her husband and two kids (who have since left the nest but not her heart). When she's not writing she spends too much of her time trying to wrangle her stubborn 2 year old dog, who likes to menace the cat and anyone who has the misfortune to visit the house.

Her previous novels include *Her Last Secret*, and *String Dolls*, both of which are available on Amazon.

www.ingramcontent.com/pod-product-compliance
Ingram Content Group UK Ltd.
Pitfield, Milton Keynes, MK11 3LW, UK
UKHW041635190726
13854UKWH00006B/2501

9 798218 926861